# BITTER VICTORY

# BITTER VICTORY

## MARY LOU HAGEN

iUniverse, Inc.
Bloomington

# BITTER VICTORY

*iUniverse books may be ordered through booksellers or by contacting:*

*iUniverse*
*1663 Liberty Drive*
*Bloomington, IN 47403*
*www.iuniverse.com*
*1-800-Authors (1-800-288-4677)*

*ISBN: 978-1-4697-7199-1 (sc)*
*ISBN: 978-1-4697-7200-4 (ebk)*

*Printed in the United States of America*

*iUniverse rev. date: 03/28/2012*

This book is dedicated to The Reverend Elder McCants and Charlene Ives Nelson. Their encouragement and faith in my writing abilities enforced my perseverance and bolstered my flagging efforts. It is to their credit that *Bitter Victory* became a published novel.

Pursue peace with all people, and holiness, without which no one will see the Lord: looking carefully lest anyone fall short of the grace of God; lest any root of bitterness springing up cause trouble, and by this many become defiled. Hebrews 12:14,15

# AUTHOR'S NOTE

WHEN MY NOVEL, *Tarnished Honor*, was published, I was delighted with the reviews and acceptance the book received. At the same time, I felt sad because I had lived with the characters for months and they were real to me. It was if they had entered my life, we became friends, and then they disappeared. I did not want to do a sequel. It's hard to explain why. Their story had been told for a brief period in their lives, and I wanted my readers to continue it themselves.

The research for *Tarnished Honor* was extensive, and much of the information I collected was not used. Almost without realizing it, ideas were floating around in my head for a similar book. The Reconstruction Era in Texas was a fascinating, if violent, period in the state's history.

Although most Texans supported and fought for the Confederacy, there was a significant number that did not favor secession and joined the Union Army.

Since the protagonist in *Tarnished Honor* was a loyal Texan and had served in the Confederate Army, I wanted to bring out another side of the conflict and its aftermath.

I chose to write the story of a Texan who went north to defend and preserve the United States. When he returns home two years after the war, he finds a different Texas than the one he left. Bitterness, hatred, violence, hardship, and conflict are raging all through the South, but never more so than in Texas.

Much of the unrest centered on the freed slaves and their struggle to be accepted as a free people. The issues of employment and education were foremost in the fight for equality. The Freemen's Bureau played a vital role in representing the Negroes and their new found rights. The Bureau enforced labor contracts and worked with religious and charitable organizations to establish schools. Teachers were recruited, mostly from the North, and they were confronted with anger and oftentimes violence.

The struggle for the rights that are guaranteed for all citizens by The United States Constitution continued long after the period written about in this book. The reader may want to compare it with the present day world.

How much progress has civilization really made?

# THE TIME OF THE KLAN

THE KLAN WAS BORN DURING the restless days after the Civil War, when time was out of joint in the South and the social order was battered and turned upside down. As a secret, nocturnal organization operating during lawless times, the Klan soon turned into a vigilante force. To restore order meant returning the Negro to the field—just as long as he didn't do too well there—and the prewar leaders to their former seats of power. Those who felt differently would have to go. And so the masked Klansmen rode out across the land. Where intimidation was not sufficient, violence was used. The Klan raided solitary cabins and invaded towns, preferably at night, but in the daytime where necessary. Although Klansmen were occasionally hurt, the death toll of Negros and Republicans probably ran close to a thousand.

The local dens proved uncontrollable and continued to operate for private as well as public ends, even after Imperial Wizard, Nathan Bedford Forrest, formally disbanded the Klan in 1869. Changing conditions and martial law finally combined to bring the Invisible Empire to an end by 1871, but the memory of the Ku Klux Klan remained as one of the treasured folk myths of the South.

There were not enough regular army forces stationed in the South. Most of the soldiers were in Texas and the rest were kept in camp, off the streets and out of the country side.

By 1869, the Klan was both increasingly successful and in serious internal trouble. A secret masked society, composed of autonomous units, dedicated to the use of force, operating in unsettled times, proved impossible to control. The better citizens were dropping out and the quality of membership in many of the states was declining. The Imperial Wizard, Forrest, ordered the dissolution of the order and the burning of all its records. His explanation was that the Klan had become perverted in some localities and that public opinion was becoming unfavorable toward masked orders. The records were destroyed but the Klan continued to operate in secret for many years afterward.

*The History of the Klu Klux Klan* by David M. Chalmers, copyright Franklin Watts, 1965

# REFERENCES

*Time of Hope, Time of Despair* by James M. Smallwood, National University Publications, copyright 1981

*The Freedmen's Bureau and Black Texans,* Barry A. Crouch, University of Texas Press, copyright 1992

*Under Their Own Vine and Fig Tree,* by William E. Montgomery, Louisiana State University Press, copyright 1992

## INCIDENTS INVOLVING THE FREEDMEN'S BUREAU

In 1867, the Freedmen's Bureau at its peak had only 59 sub-assistant commissioners and 10 assistant subagents in Texas, a total too small to perform effectively its work because of the huge size of the state.

Thomas Blackshear, a planter, tired of what he termed black loafers closed his contract with freedmen and rented land to Anglos after his Negro tenants refused to help him slaughter his hogs. Dissatisfaction with proposed pay, extremely cold weather and the fact that the work was extra explained their refusal, but Blackshear saw only laziness.

Further, he maintained that the other planters in his area, after having had similar experiences intended to replace freedmen. Concurrently, smaller planters and farmers who adjusted to a free labor system more easily because they depended less on Negro labor, either hired white hands, or performed more of their work. Most employers who had relied on black labor before the war however, continued to do so. Desperate for cheap labor, some paid agents to recruit freedmen in other Southern states who were willing to immigrate to Texas. At the same time, to ensure their control over Negro labor they joined associations that established guidelines for wages and pledged themselves not to hire another employer's black workers.

The Bureau always lacked the manpower needed to police the entire state and, unless directly threatened by the presence of a garrison, or at least the presence of a subagent, local law enforcement officers and courts often defied Kiddo and obeyed their legislature. General Griffin reissued the order voiding the labor code. Griffin enlarged the Bureau and sent agents into what had been untouched regions, many whites still resisted federal authority, obeying only when forced.

A Bureau agent, who traveled through the interior of the state from Austin to Tyler to assume command of the Bureau post there, added his testimony to that of others. All along his route, freedmen besieged him, swearing that neither their property nor lives were safe and begging him to stay and protect them. After reaching Tyler, the agent found that similar conditions existed there.

Other Anglos hired men, considered outlaws by federal officials, who performed Klan work. In the pay of Bowie County landowners, supported by local whites who identified him with the Lost Cause, the notorious Cullen Baker would kill any freedman for a few dollars. He did not hesitate to shoot . . . (freedmen) on the slightest complaint made by the employers." Further, Baker assaulted blacks if they sought Bureau protection. Similarly, Dave Timmins of Titus County retained a local band of outlaws to intimidate laborers. Apparently, a large group of Anglos in Wood, Hunt and Van Zandt counties supported the Ben Bickerstiff gang, because it "specialized in attacking freedmen and driving them from their crops." While Bickerstaff committed his depredations, another "concert of organization . . . among outlaws" in the Jefferson area attacked Negros, forcing them off their lands.

Freedmen in the Brenham suburb of Watersville (Watrousville), a segregated shanty town, built a community center that met the religious needs of all denominations and also served as the headquarters for the Loyal League.

In 1867 in Palestine whites stoned a Negro church, forced its congregation and its Anglo minister into the street and warned the preacher that if he wanted to speak to freedmen again, he could give his next sermon in hell.

In 1867, many doctors in Freestone County refused treatment to all Negroes, and whites as well, who belonged to the Loyal League. Because of the shortage of doctors, the inability of freedmen to pay fees, and the refusal of some physicians to treat them, blacks tended to rely on druggists for patent remedies and often received drugs that did not improve their condition.

White doctors and druggists sometimes added to the Negroes' problems. Most Anglo physicians would treat freedmen who could afford their fee, but political tensions influenced some to use their positions to control blacks.

In 1867, General Charles Griffin forbade segregation on common carriers. Local agents intervened in civil affairs when whites applied laws to blacks unjustly.

## THE KLU KLUX KLAN

The Klan was born during the restless days after the Civil War, when time was out of joint in the South and the social order was battered and turned upside down.

They came in the night . . . . The men were bearded and their clothing dirty and stained. Their expressions were grimaced, the dust spooled up in their wake as they galloped toward a place that had had already been drenched in blood, a place where the terrible battle had ended, a place of death.

*The History of the Klu Klux Klan* by David M. Chalmers, copyright Franklin Watts, 1965

# ADDAGES, PROVERBS, QUOTES, ETC.

W E DO NOT STRUGGLE IN despair but in hope, not from doubt but from faith, not from hate but out of love for ourselves and our humanity. (Robert Flemington's tale "A Crisis of Faith." Black Theologian James Cone)

Memories of de bad times keep on livin' . . . They can live a long time, like a ol' dog long as we feed dem in dey cages. Ex-slave. Equality is difficult, but superiority is painful. African Serere Ephesians Ch. 4:31-32.

Let all bitterness and wrath, and anger, and glamour, and evil speaking, be put away from you, with all malice: and be ye kind to one another, tenderhearted, forgiving one another, even as God for Christ's sake hath forgiven you.

In 1867, a group of freed slaves gathered at the edge of Brenham and formed a settlement called Waterstown. They established a church and a school.

In 1867, from March to December there were 175 murders and 225 assaults by whites against blacks. Seventy-eight in December alone. (This was reported in the Corsicana area.)

In 1867, there were 57 local Freedmen posts and 69 subagents.

Vivian captured in August 1867. Other known criminals were Cullen Baker and Bill Bateman (reported in Bowie County).

*Mary Lou Hagen*

## GRIMES COUNTY LANDMARKS AND PLACES OF BUINESS

Anderson Buffington Hotel

Becker-Steinhagen House—furniture and household goods

Jennings House

Dr. Parker home and office

Baptist Church Native stone. Great grandfather of LBJ was minister from 1852-1861

Steinhagen furniture and cabinet

Bay House saddle and harness maker

Bay Grocery W. E. Bay

La Prelle Hotel John LaPrell

Sally Johnson School

New York Row House

*The Army in Texas During Reconstruction*
by William L. Richter, copyright 1984

1867

When Richard Harris was charged with assault with intent to kill in Grimes County, he fled to de Gress, a former Union brevet colonel subassistant commissioner, whose office was in Houston.

Harris received the agent's protection. Governor Throckmorton invited de Gress to withdraw from the case, but the colonel replied in such a disrespectful manner that he caused the governor to ask for his court martial by the Adjutant General's Office in Washington. Throckmorton denied de Gress' charge that he did not have all the facts; he pledged to uphold all state and federal laws in the case but received no satisfaction.

The frequent requests for soldiers to assist state courts and to protect Loyalists and freedmen, led to encounters with irate citizens. On an expedition to Navasota to arrest two men charged with the murder of soldiers, First Lieutenant William A. Sutherland and his company of infantrymen were blocked by a crowd of 30 or 40 men. Sutherland gave a quick order to surround the citizens group and then demanded that the civilians surrender their weapons. He was careful not to search anybody or allow his men to roam the streets while in town even though it compromised his mission. Later a citizen wrote an apology to Governor Throckmorton for the town's action, blaming it on drunks and rowdies.

In July, 1867, Congress passed a third Reconstruction Act, which authorized military commanders to remove any civil officer who obstructed the Reconstruction process. About the same time, Sheridan forwarded all of Griffin warnings to Grant in Washington, noting that Griffin "attributes this condition of affairs to a disloyal governor and his subordinate civil officeholders." In late July, Grant wrote Sheridan the power to fill the vacancies with appointments of his choice.

Sheridan did not delay in exercising his authority. "A careful consideration of the reports of Brevet Major General Charles Griffin," Sheridan decreed, "shows that J. W. Throckmorton, Governor of Texas, is an impediment to the reconstruction of the State, under the law; he is therefore removed from office." Sheridan appointed Elisha M. Pease as the new provisional governor—the man who had overwhelmingly lost the election that had placed "Throcky," as the Republicans now derisively called him, in office one year before. At ten o'clock in the morning, August 8, 1867, Elisha M. Pease took over the governor's chair.

September, 1867

Then came an unexpected interruption: the entire Gulf Coast was inundated by yellow fever. Galveston was without doctors, as nearly all civilian and military doctors succumbed to the disease. Griffin's own family contracted the illness. The general himself fell ill and succumbed to the disease.

The general's death was a grievous blow to Reconstruction in Texas. With his passing, the Republicans lost their chance to work with an understanding, cooperative officer to install their men into office before Hancock's conservative influence could be felt.

Because of the yellow fever epidemic, army command changes and new registration guidelines, the election originally scheduled for November, 1867, was postponed until February, 1868; this delay was partly responsible for the eventual Republican victory.

There were claims that over 100 cases of homicide had occurred in 1867. (Benjamin C. Truman asserted that Texas averaged over 450 murders each year before the Civil War.) The figure of 100 cases could not be verified because the proclamation took effect in December, 1866.

In 1867, the U. S. Department of Education was established to collect information on schools and teaching them to help the States to establish effective school systems. Each state representative held an institute in his district. Abram Shortridge, editor of The Educationalist and president of the Indianapolis schools was among the instructors. State Librarian John Clark Redpathand and faculty members of the State University and private normal schools were also instructors.

# MARY LOU HAGEN

# Biography

BORN AND REARED IN INDIANA, Mary Lou Hagen has had a love affair with the Old West since she was a child. Educated at Indiana and Purdue Universities, a career change in 1985 brought her to San Antonio. She remained in Texas and lives with her Yorkie-Terrier mix, Daisy.

Mrs. Hagen is particularly interested in historical fiction Her previous works include *Texas Widow,* and *Gambler's Widow,* both based on a true story, *Tarnished Honor,* and a *A Taste of Texas,* also based on a true story.

# CHAPTER ONE

*Fort Riley, Kansas, February 1867*

T HE TWO MEN SHOOK HANDS. "I'm sorry you decided to leave the
army, Trace," the older of the two men said. He wore gold bars on his
shoulders and the United States cavalry insignia on his blue coat.

"I know sir, but you know how I sweated over the decision," the man
with the sergeant's stripes answered.

"Yes, I know it didn't come easy. I'm sure you feel ready for the
repercussions you'll face when you get back to Texas. But hatred runs deep
and this nation will be many years in overcoming it, if it ever does."

\*    \*    \*

*Anderson, Texas*

Trace Burdette climbed down from the stage and surveyed his
surroundings. Dusty streets, worn boardwalks and weather-beaten
buildings. Yep, he was back in Texas, all right. After a six-year absence,
nothing on the surface seemed to have changed.

For the most part, the little crowd that had gathered to watch the
stage arrive was silent. There was a wary look in their eyes and not a sign
of welcome on their faces. He was glad he had purchased civilian clothes
and put his uniform in the bottom of the large carpetbag he took from the
driver. One or two men in the crowd looked familiar but he wasn't sure
of their names. During the war, he had met many men from other areas
of the country and their faces had replaced the ones at home. Home! He

was finally home after years of bloody cavalry charges, exploding artillery shells and painful saber wounds. There was no welcoming committee to greet the man who had chosen to grind the Stars and Bars into the dust and carry the Union standard to victory.

The crowd parted and he stepped onto the boardwalk. The stage had stopped in front of the Anderson Hotel. He noted the Fanthrop Inn was still in business. The Fanthrops were staunch Confederates. Their only son had died shortly after enlisting in the Confederate Army.

"Burdette!" A gruff voice called from behind.

Trace turned to see a man in overalls and heavy work shoes striding toward him. His unshaven face with heavy eyebrows over narrowed eyes was neither friendly nor hostile. He stopped within a foot of Trace and looked him up and down.

"I wondered if you would come back when Alvin died."

Trace studied the man's features and a name came to him. "Collins, Fred Collins, isn't it? You were my pa's friend."

"That's right. And you broke his heart when you joined them blue bellies to fight against us. He never got over having a son turn traitor."

Trace held his temper in check. He had expected this when he decided to return to Texas. "The war is over, Collins. Best lay it to rest."

Collins grinned but no merriment showed in his eyes or in his voice. "Yeah, 'spect that would be best—for you, anyway. But you better be ready to hear and feel it ain't."

Without responding, Trace walked into the hotel. He thought about his plans to take over the farm that had gone to his brother when his parents died. Now that Alvin was gone, it was his property. Was it worth the sacrifice of a promising military career?

He strode into the hotel lobby. The worn furnishings and even more worn carpet had seen better days. Trace did not recognize the young woman behind the scarred desk. Her shiny brown hair was pulled back from her face and pinned in a topknot of curls.

"Good afternoon. May I help you, sir?"

"Yes, ma'am. I need a room for tonight." He placed the carpetbag on the floor and signed his name in the book that lay facing him.

Turning the register around, she read his signature.

"T. R. Burdette," she whispered. Her head lifted and she stared at him, a shocked look on her face.

"Yes, ma'am. Is something wrong?" His voice held an edge, a result of Collin's comments.

"Oh, no. It's just that . . . that I . . . I knew a young man named Burdette. He died three weeks ago."

The hard look in Trace's eyes matched the expression on his face. "I think you're referring to my brother, ma'am. Alvin Burdette."

"You're Alvin's brother? The one who fought for the Yankees?" It was a question, without a hint of condemnation.

"Yes, I'm the traitor." Irony saturated his words.

She shook her head. "Oh, no, Mr. Burdette. I don't think that at all and neither did Alvin."

"How do you know that?"

"He told me so."

"Well, my Pa certainly did and I thought Alvin did too, although he never said so."

"You know Alvin was too young to go to war when it all began. He said he was glad he didn't have to make that decision with your father feeling one way and you another."

"We didn't talk about it much before I left. I was never sure how Alvin felt." Trace recalled his brother's questions about why the country wanted to tear itself apart, and that he, Trace, had no answers the young boy would understand.

"He didn't blame you."

Trace glanced at the woman's left hand, which was bare of a wedding band. "I'm sorry I don't remember you, ma'am. You must have been pretty young when I left."

"My name is Anne Michaels. We moved here during the war. My father owns the hotel. I met Alvin at a church social. We became friends. He . . . he . . . ," the young woman's voice faltered.

Trace nodded. He found it hard to believe his brother was gone. First, his mother died early in the war and his father followed two years later. When Trace decided to remain in the army after the war ended, Alvin kept the farm going. He pushed the thoughts to the back of his mind. "If I could have my key?"

"Yes, of course. Room 101. It's at the head of the stairs, first door on the left." She picked a key from the board behind her, turned and offered it to him.

3

"Thanks." Trace picked up his carpetbag and headed toward the stairway.

*    *    *

The fancy sign read Joseph E. Hutcheson, *Attorney at Law.* Loyal to the Confederacy, *Joe Hutcheson* had fought with Stonewall Jackson. Once the war was over, he saw the need to put the past behind him. He remained in the east and studied law at the University of Virginia. Trace knew Joe was probably the only person in Anderson that did not hold a grudge.

Hutcheson was on his feet before Trace reached his office.

"I heard you were in town, Mr. Burdette." The lawyer held out his hand.

Hutcheson's grip was firm. Trace searched his face for some sign of condemnation but found none.

"Yeah, I came back to clear up a few matters."

Hutcheson pointed to one of the two chairs in front of his desk. "Have a seat." He sat down behind the desk and pulled a large envelope from a drawer. "These are all the documents pertaining to the homestead. I don't know if you were aware of it, but your father made a will after you left."

"My mother wrote me a few times before she died. She said Pa was going to leave the farm to Alvin."

"He did, but Alvin made a will. There are some papers for you to sign and a few details to take care of, and the homestead is yours. You're lucky, sir, Alvin managed to keep the place free of debt. You can get a good price for it."

Trace's lips tightened. He hesitated. Might as well come out with it. "I don't plan to sell."

Joe's eyes widened and he leaned forward in his chair.

He was silent for a moment before he spoke. "Don't misunderstand me, Mr. Burdett. I have no feelings of animosity toward you at all. I think you followed your conscience and did what you felt you had to do. When the war was over, I saw the necessity of putting prejudice aside. The country needed to rebuild and it would take trained men to move the process along. That's when I decided to go law school. Although there are more difficult times ahead, I have no doubt our great country can stand the test." The lawyer's face colored as he said, "I didn't mean to get on my soap box."

He continued. "When you stayed in the army, folks just naturally thought you would never come back. Then Alvin died, and I was duty bound to try to locate you. I'm glad I did."

"There's been talk that the place would be sold for taxes. Of course, I have said nothing."

There was no mirth in the grin that flashed across Trace's stern features. "Kind of a joke, don't you think? The place already owned by a Yankee sympathizer? Or maybe I'll be called a carpetbagger."

*     *     *

"He looks sound, enough." Trace ran his hands over the grey gelding's muscular thighs.

"He is. You know I don't sell nags," the livery owner answered. Don Simpson had owned the livery when Trace was a boy.

"Yeah. You didn't before I went away." Trace did not feel the need to say more.

Simpson looked at him, his eyes narrowed. "Still don't. Who you fought for and why don't have nothin' to do with it."

"I'm glad you feel that way. And since most people don't, I wonder if you would mind telling me about Alvin and how he died. The letter from the lawyer said the he was killed in some kind of accident."

Simpson hesitated, shifting the tobacco cud in his mouth. His voice was flat when he answered. "Fred Collins found him in the field, the lines still wrapped around his hands and the horse gone. There was a bloody gash on his forehead and blood on some rocks close to the body."

Trace stared at Simpson. "Fred Collins found Alvin?"

"Yeah. Works part time at the feed store and went to deliver some feed. Guess Alvin was trying to get some early plowin' done and something' spooked the horse."

Trace's brow furrowed. "That's funny. He didn't mention it when he hailed me down yesterday."

"I don't know 'bout that. Sheriff investigated and it was ruled an accident."

Trace was silent for a moment, turning the story over in his mind. "Do *you* think it was an accident?"

"I don't know any more than I've told you. Now, do you want the horse or not?"

Trace held back the urge to tell Simpson that he could keep his horses, but Trace knew he would not get a fair deal anyplace else. "Yeah, I'll take him and some used gear if you've got any."

*   *   *

Spring arrives early in Texas. The mesquite trees displayed their feathery leaves and the pastures resembled yards of green carpet interspersed with budding bluebonnets. Indian paintbrush and a myriad of other colorful wildflowers were poking their heads through the ground. Some of the fields had been plowed, the rich dark earth waiting to nourish the seeds that would soon be planted. In his mind's eye, Trace could see the rows of cotton, the bowls bursting with the white gold that was the backbone of the South. Tiny green shoots peeped through the short rows laid out in a small field. Evidently, some of the farmers had found the money to put in crops. With that thought came the reminder of Alvin. Trace spurred the grey gelding into a lope. He wanted to see his home and find the place where his brother died.

The lane leading up to the farmhouse was overgrown with weeds and brush. It opened into a wide clearing, and Trace felt a lump form in his throat. Made of split logs and chinked with mud, the house stood straight and tall. Originally, two cabins connected by a dog run, the house had been enlarged as time passed, but the dog run had never been enclosed. It provided a place to rest from the hot Texas sun and catch the endless Texas breeze. As he drew closer, Trace could see the signs of neglect. The chinking was gone in several places and shingles were missing from the split cedar roof. Several panes of glass were missing from the windows. Trace stayed in the saddle, his eyes roving over the place where he had spent the first nineteen years of his life. The well where his mother had drawn water, the outbuildings made of logs, the entrance to the cellar; all brought long buried memories to the surface. He grinned when he remembered the times he had been told to wait in the barn to be punished for some misdeed he had committed. Pa was not a strict disciplinarian, but he did not hesitate to use the strap when Trace and Alvin disobeyed him.

Dismounting, stiff from the unaccustomed saddle, Trace shook his head at the thought of the Army's famous McClellan. New troopers found it an instrument of torture and old timers pointed to the calluses on their backsides. He removed his black Stetson and wiped his brow. The Texas sun was like no other. Even in the spring, a man raised a sweat when exposed to its direct rays. Looping the reins over a low hanging branch, Trace walked toward the house.

The door was unlocked, which did not surprise Trace. His family had never locked their doors. Waiting until his eyes adjusted to the dim light, Trace stood on the threshold. Dust particles danced in the sunshine filtering through the windows. His boot heels sounded hollow as he stepped into the large room that served as kitchen, dining room and sitting room. A heavy layer of dust covered the pine floorboards. The large oak table sat in the middle of the room just as it had when he was growing up. He counted four chairs where there used to be six. His eyes took in the old pie safe and the heavy cast iron range. Trace wondered if somebody had been keeping an eye on the place. Not the army, although Texans depended more on the military for protection than the local authorities. Political upheaval placed heavy restrictions on law enforcement agencies.

A close inspection of the house revealed no sign of recent occupancy. Trace found no extensive damage and to the best of his recollection, the furniture was intact. When he examined the trunks where his mother had kept clothing and linens, he found them empty. A keen sense of loss invaded his senses. He remembered his mother sewing shirts for her men folk. How she loved the quilting bees that resulted in the pretty quilts on their beds.

Trace stood in the empty house while memories crowded his mind and dulled his senses. Coming out of his reverie, he sensed another presence in the room. Turning, he saw that a big shaggy dog had joined him. It stood, watching him with wary eyes.

"Now where did you come from?" Trace took a step forward and the dog retreated a step backward.

"It's alright boy, I won't hurt you." Trace held out his hand, palm up.

The dog backed away. It was thin but not emaciated, and its eyes were a clear brown ringed in black. The animal suddenly turned and bolted for the door. Trace followed and watched as it ran across the yard and disappeared into the trees. Some gut instinct told him it might be a good idea to follow the dog. Before he could put his thoughts into action, Trace felt his stomach rumble. A slight hunger pang reminded him it was past the nooning hour. He had a couple of biscuits from breakfast stashed in his saddlebags and if he could draw some water from the well, it would do until suppertime.

To his surprise, there was a bucket attached to the well rope. Trace lowered it and brought up a bucket of water. *That's strange. Looks like there should be some debris on the surface unless somebody's somebody has been using the well regular like.*

Trace shrugged. *There's bound to be travelers passin' by and needin' water.* He had read in the northern newspapers about the homeless Confederate soldiers, roaming bands of freed slaves and lawless men that prayed on the countryside.

After tending his horse and polishing off the biscuits, Trace took up the dog's trail. Not trusting an unscrupulous traveler who might steal the gelding, he led the animal into the woods. A few yards into the trees, a cleared field came into view. Part of it had been plowed but the majority lay fallow.

Was this the field where Alvin had died? How many times had he, Trace, tilled corn in this field—corn that was taken to the mill and ground into meal to make the family's daily bread?

For some reason, coming home was harder than Trace had anticipated. He could see his father's face the day he left. There were no accusations, no angry words, just the sadness in his father's eyes. And his mother. She had hugged him tight, her voice choked with tears that soaked the front of his shirt.

\*     \*     \*

"Oh, son," she sobbed. "Why are you doing this? Texas is your home. Your granddaddy fought Indians and all kinds of hardships to claim the land for his children and grandchildren."

Trace smoothed the top of her hair. "I know that, Mama. I'll always be proud of my roots, but . . . We don't have slaves, never did have. I have to follow my conscience, and if I stay here, I will be bound to fight for the Confederacy. I can't do that, Mama. You know we've talked and talked. Now it's time for me to go."

Alvin stood, watching the exchange between his parents and his brother. He was twelve years old and he did not understand any of it. Trace stepped out of his mother's arms and turned to Alvin. The brothers shook hands. Trace saw a tear in the corner of Alvin's eye and watched it trickle slowly down his cheek.

\*    \*    \*

The dog suddenly appeared in Trace's line of vision. It stood on the other side of the field at the edge of the woods. Leading the gelding, Trace started across the field.

His boot heels sunk in the soft ground and made the short distance seem much further. No cavalryman liked to walk when he could ride. The dog did not bark but continued to watch him. When man and dog were about ten feet apart, the animal bolted back into the woods.

An unseen force propelled Trace to follow the dog. He tied the gelding to a low hanging limb and pulled his pistol from his saddlebag. Four years of war had taught him to keep his guard up.

A small stream wound its way through the woods. He knew it originated from a spring a half mile away. An overgrown path ran along the side of the creek. The dog had disappeared and Trace took the path to the right toward the spring. A stone's throw from the mouth of the creek stood a crude lean-to built of young saplings and roofed with weathered canvas. Trace raised his arm, the pistol ready to fire.

"Anybody here?"

Silence enveloped the area. There was no sign of life. Trace walked toward the shelter, his eyes taking in signs of recent occupancy. A fire ring had been built in front of the lean-to, the stones blackened from numerous fires. He squatted and put his fingers in the ashes. Cold. From his position, he could see inside the shelter. There appeared to be some blankets or remnants of bedding. Trace came to his feet. Somebody had been camping here and he intended to find out who and why.

# CHAPTER TWO

*March 1867*
*Indianapolis, Indiana*

"**A**s you know, Miss Mills, the American Missionary Society is in dire need of teachers, especially in Texas. Not many men want to go there, to say nothing of young women. I will not deceive you; it is a violent and lawless place. Texas has not rejoined the Union and is under martial law. Local law enforcement, in most instances, is lax. I must impress upon you the risks you would be taking. Of course, we will do everything we can to protect you, but we cannot guarantee your safety."

The young woman sat facing the recruiting director of the Society. She listened intently as Mr. Rutledge emphasized what she could encounter if she accepted a teaching position in Texas. Her gloved hands were folded in her lap, her legs crossed at the ankles under full skirts; a picture of proper decorum. Her teaching credentials were impeccable; a certificate from Indiana Female College, and two years of teaching experience in a Christian school. She had attended the state required teachers' institutes each fall. Organized and developed by the well known educator, Caleb Mills, and the State school system, they were under the supervision of learned scholars. Abram Shortridge, editor of the publication, The Educationalist, and president of the Indianapolis public schools, State Librarian John Clark Redpath, faculty members of the State University and private normal schools served on the governing board. The institutes provided the teachers with the opportunity to further their education. That fact added to her eligibility. She was more than qualified to teach in a frontier school.

Rutledge noted she lived with an older brother and his wife in a good neighborhood in the city. He wondered if she might be related to Caleb Mills.

"I am aware of the situation, Mr. Rutledge. I have been reading the articles written by Miss Frances Harper. She is a very talented writer, and I believe she is telling the truth."

"Oh, yes, I am acquainted with Miss Harper. She is a fine woman as well as a gifted writer."

"There is another aspect in my favor, Mr. Rutledge. My paternal uncle and his wife have lived in Texas for many years. There is no bitterness between us, and I am sure they would welcome me into their home. Of course, since I do not know where you would assign me, it probably would be a temporary arrangement. It's not as if I were going there without support of any kind."

Mr. Rutledge nodded his head. "Yes, that is certainly an advantage. But, and pardon me if I seem to be prying into your personal life, but why would a young woman like yourself from a . . . a privileged background, want to leave the North? I know your late father was an educator, and your brother is the assistant principal at The Christian Academy.

Regina Mills smiled, showing even white teeth. Stray curls of light brown hair peaked from under a matching bonnet. She smoothed the folds in her navy blue skirt.

"No, you are not prying, sir. It is rather difficult to explain. You see, my mother died several years ago and when my father passed away last year, my brother and his wife did not want me to live alone in our family home. They insisted I live with them. I agreed. I do have a small inheritance, which gives me a modicum of independence. Although my sister-in-law and I get along very well; she has been most gracious and kind, I . . . Well, I have always wanted to . . . to do more with my life."

The recruiter nodded. "I think I understand what you are saying." He cleared his throat. "Miss Mills I would like to discuss the salary arrangements. The present salary paid by the Freedmen's Bureau is forty dollars per month. The Society pays a stipend of fifteen dollars per month but, unfortunately, that amount is deducted from the salary paid by the Bureau. Teachers are allowed to keep the tuition fees. At present, the fee is fifty cents per month per student. If there are two students in the family, the fee is seventy-five cents with a maximum of one dollar. The fees have been waived for widows and orphans. The Society will, of course pay your transportation costs to Texas. We also provide you with teaching materials and supplies. I must emphasize the amounts may change from time to time. It depends on how much the parents can pay."

Regina nodded, thinking of her income from the trust. It was a comfort to know that she would have additional funds if she needed them. "The arrangement sounds satisfactory. I don't foresee any problems in that area."

Mr. Rutledge's expression relayed his relief. "Good. The Society will meet next week to discuss the applicants we have interviewed. I am sure you will be asked to come again and talk with the board members. As far as I am concerned, you have my vote."

Regina's face beamed. She rose from her chair and Mr. Rutledge was on his feet immediately. He came around the desk and took the hand she offered.

"Thank you, Mr. Rutledge. I appreciate your confidence in me. I'll look forward to hearing from you."

\*     \*     \*

"What?" exclaimed David Mills. "You can't be serious?" The man's face colored and he stood up from the dining room table, his eyes glaring at his sister.

"Now David, let Regina finish before you lose your temper." Nancy Mills cautioned.

"Yes, David, please hear me out."

David sat down, his posture rigid. "All right. But I will tell you right now, I will not give my permission for you to leave your home to go to that God forsaken place. You have been reading too many of that Harper woman's tall tales."

"I am twenty-two years old. I do not need your permission, *David.*" Regina felt the flush spread over her face and neck at the heated tone in her voice. Had not Nancy told her she must handle the situation with the utmost care? She seemed to understand Regina's need for a life of her own apart from her family.

She ignored her brother's caustic comment about Frances Harper. "I will admit there is risk involved, but there are risks in everything one undertakes. Besides, it's not as if we do not have family there."

David scowled and his voice held an edge. "Family, yes, but we have never been close to Uncle Edward and his wife. Why, I don't recall ever meeting them but one time when they came back to Indiana before Grandfather passed on. They seemed . . . well a bit crude. I guess that comes from living on the frontier among savages."

"I am sure their life has not been one of luxury, but they do own a sizeable farm in Texas. In her last letter, Aunt Martha mentioned they had hired several freed slaves to help them with the planting."

David's face colored. "I know it must be difficult for them having lost both their sons in the war."

Nancy spoke for the first time since David's initial outburst. "Yes, it is a tragedy and perhaps a visit from family would help ease their pain a bit."

"I hardly think you could call a period of two year's a *visit.*" The irony in David's voice was not lost on Regina.

"Mr. Rutledge assured me that if circumstances make it impossible for me to continue teaching, the contract will be canceled," she explained.

"That in itself is evidence enough of how dangerous it is," David snapped.

The door between the dining room and kitchen opened a fraction and a head appeared. Nancy, upon spying the maid, used the opportunity to break up the discussion. "You may bring in the dessert now, Hannah."

\*　　\*　　\*

There was no further discussion of Regina's trip to Texas. David had forbidden her to go and, as far as he was concerned, the subject was closed. The young woman dreaded the confrontation to come, but she was going to accept a position if it was offered. Frances Harper continued to write of the unrest and violence occurring throughout the South.

The women were careful to talk about Regina's decision only in the privacy of her bedroom. "You know I will support you in any way I can although you realize my efforts must be discrete." Nancy was an attractive woman with brown hair and eyes offset by a flawless complexion.

Regina smiled. "I know and I do not want to do anything that would cause trouble between you and David. You have both been very kind, taking me into your home where I have felt most welcome."

Nancy crossed the room to her sister-in-law's side and embraced her. "This is your home for as long as you want it to be. But I understand why you want to go to Texas, and I will worry about you and keep you in my prayers."

*   *   *

A few days later, Regina was summoned to the Society office. It was imperative that she make the best possible impression. She dressed carefully, choosing a modest dove gray gown with a full skirt and a fitted basque which buttoned up the front to a white lace collar.

Mr. Rutledge met her in the outer office and escorted her to the conference room. He introduced the five gentlemen in the room. Regina hid her surprise to discover two of the men were Negroes.

Regina recognized young Mr. Fairbanks. His picture appeared in the newspaper quite often.

He was becoming quite the politician She had met Mr. Shortridge when she attended the Institute.

"I know your brother quite well, Miss Mills," Mr. Shortridge said. "I'm surprised he would give his permission for you to go to Texas to teach."

Regina smiled. "David was not in favor of it, but I finally convinced him it is something I feel I must do."

After several comments and questions, one of the men brought up the subject of living arrangements. "Are you aware, Miss Mills, there can be problems with finding appropriate housing?"

Regina hesitated. "Yes, I believe Mr. Rutledge did mention that could be difficult. I am prepared to pay additional compensation for good accommodations."

"Er a err, it is not the cost involved that is the problem. I am going to be blunt, Miss Mills. The problem is whether any of the local people will be willing to take you in. It is no secret that Southerners resent what we are trying to accomplish. Their loyalty to the Confederacy was not buried with their soldiers at Gettysburg." The man's voice and expression were grim.

The silence grew as Regina gathered her thoughts. What could she say that would ease Mr. Fairbanks' mind? She picked her words with care.

"I've weighed the pros and cons and thought about my decision very carefully. There may be danger and disappointment, but I am a Christian, and I believe faith is my strongest weapon."

The men exchanged glances and nodded approvingly. Mr. Rutledge stood and announced that she would hear the board's decision in a week or two.

The letter arrived a week later. She had been accepted! The train for Texas would depart in two weeks time. Nancy was almost as excited as Regina. "From what Aunt Martha has written, the weather in Texas is very changeable. The winters are not as cold and long as they are here".

Regina laughed. "But she said the summers are as hot as Hades."

"Well, that means that you will need a variety of clothing. Let's start with what you will need when you leave. You know, you can always send for things later." Nancy opened the big armoire and began removing articles of clothing.

Regina and Nancy managed to keep the departure date from David until three days before Regina was to leave. The matter came to a head without warning.

Dinner was a quiet meal. David seemed preoccupied. The women followed his lead. Regina's mood grew somber as she glanced at the lovely table setting. The linen tablecloth and Nancy's second best china, crystal and flatware were most likely far more elegant than anything she would find in Texas.

Dessert was finished and the table cleared, before David spoke. "Regina please come into the study. We have something that needs addressing." Not waiting for the ladies to rise, he stood and left the room.

"Oh, dear," Nancy whispered, "he knows."

"He had to find out some time." Regina braced herself for the confrontation.

"Remember, I'm with you. I will be in the parlor if you need me."

"Thank you, Nancy, but I see no need for you to be dragged into this." Her head high and her posture rigid, Regina followed her brother into the study.

David stood with his back to the room in front of the windows which overlooked the back garden. She could tell by the set of his shoulders that he was trying to control his anger.

"David, I know you have my best interests at heart, but you might as well accept the fact that I am going to Texas. I am of legal age and quite capable of making my own decisions."

David turned and faced his sister. His face was flushed but his voice was cold when he answered. "You have been sheltered and protected all your life. You have no idea what you are getting into. Texas is a wild and lawless country. They have refused all offers to rejoin the Union. They are under martial law and God only knows what kind of . . . of activities are going on there. There have been articles in the papers that . . . that . . . ," David could not go on.

"I know that. I read the papers, too."

"And you still want to go to such a place? Why, Regina, why? Are you so unhappy here that you are willing to put yourself in grave danger?"

"No, David, it has nothing to do with being unhappy. You and Nancy have been nothing but kind and loving. It's just that I feel . . . I want to go where I am needed. Really needed. The Negro people want an education, to learn to read and write. And not just the children. The adults want to go to school, too. Now that they are free, they need to prepare to look after themselves, to try to build a new life. You and I both know how important education is. We had the opportunity to learn. An opportunity that until now has been denied them. Don't you see, David, that if we who can teach do not respond to their need, we are doing them the same injustice as their former owners?"

David sighed and shook his head. "I can see your mind is made up. And, as you said, you are of legal age. We will miss you and worry about you and pray for your safety and well being."

Regina, her eyes misty from the tears she fought to hold back, ran to her brother and embraced him.

*     *     *

The train station was teaming with activity when Regina, David and Nancy arrived. Conveyances loaded with mounds of baggage were lined up, and the boardwalk crowded with men, women and children in all manner of dress. Nancy gripped Regina's arm and whispered, "Look at the people. Most of them look as if they can't wait to leave. You know, I do envy you a little, being able to make your own decisions and begin a new life for yourself." Her face colored and she added, "Oh, you know I love David with all my heart and have never regretted marrying him, but it seems so exciting to . . . to . . . ."

Regina patted her sister-in-law's hand. "I understand. When you and David have children, you will be glad you did not run off to such a wild place."

Nancy smiled, a hint of sadness in her eyes. "I know you're right. And the doctors say there is no reason we cannot have children. After all, two years is not a very long time."

The conductor announced the train would be departing in ten minutes. A flurry of activity erupted as the crowd pressed forward. With a last hug for her brother and sister-in-law, Regina hurried to join the people who were boarding the train.

Regina surveyed her fellow travelers and discovered two young Negro women and a young Negro man seated several rows ahead. From their dress and manner, she doubted they were domestic workers. Could they be teachers traveling to Texas?

The trip to St. Louis, that Regina had made with her father once before, was uncomfortable, tiresome and dirty. There were no accommodations for washing or a decent meal. Her dark green traveling suit was wrinkled and dusty long before they reached their destination.

At a stop in a small town in Illinois, Regina found herself beside the two Negro women waiting in line for a sandwich. She took a deep breath, gathered her courage and spoke.

"My name is Regina Mills. I am a teacher and I am on my way to Texas."

The young women stared at her for a moment before the taller one answered. "I am Bertha Hopper and this is my friend, Janie Sowers. We are teachers and we, too, are on our way to Texas."

Regina smiled. "Oh, that's wonderful. Mr. Rutledge told me the Society desperately needs teachers. I'm so glad there are others who are willing to teach those who really want to learn."

Regina caught the strange look that passed between the two Negro women. *Do they think I'm being condescending?* A proper young white lady would hesitate to speak on a personal level with Negroes. Regina was a lady, but she did not want the women to think she looked down on them.

Bertha's voice was even when she answered. "That's true, but it was hard to convince our parents to let us go. If my brother, Stephen, had not wanted to go to Texas, they would never have given their permission."

Regina suffered a small twinge of conscience. David had objected to her decision. "I have not received my assignment and will be going to my uncle and aunt's near Marshall, Texas. I hope I don't have to wait too long to be placed. Have you been assigned, yet?"

"Yes, we have," Bertha returned. She glanced at Janie, disappointment plain on her face.

Janie spoke for the first time. "We are being sent to different places. Bertha has been assigned to a school in Marshall. My assignment is in Corsicana. I just hope we can see each other once in awhile."

Back on the train, Regina ate her sandwich. The bread was stale and the meat, described as roast beef, was tough and stringy. She contemplated sitting with the Negroes and exchanging ideas about their teaching duties. No, one can only take so much liberty with society's rules. Perhaps in Texas it would be less restrictive.

# CHAPTER THREE

I T WAS LATE AFTERNOON WHEN Trace returned to town. Simpson had gone home and left a gimpy old cowboy in charge of the livery.

"Want me to rub 'im down and feed 'im fur ye?"

"Much obliged." Trace pitched the man two bits, took his saddlebags and rifle and headed for the hotel. He needed a good wash and a meal under his belt. The lobby was empty except for a man behind the desk.

"You Trace Burdette?" He was stocky with the beginnings of a paunch, and Trace thought that running a hotel probably didn't offer much in the way of exercise.

"Yes, I am."

In spite of his soft hands, the man's handshake was firm. "I'm John Michaels. Sorry about Alvin. Mighty sorry. He was a good young man. Him and my girl hit it right off. Thought somethin' might come of it but . . ."

"Seems like a fine young woman." Trace didn't know what else to say.

"She is. Takes after her ma. My Maurine was an angel. Lost her to the fever five years ago. Right after we moved here."

Trace could read the pain in the man's eyes and hear the sadness in his voice. Before he could respond, a voice called out.

"Papa, supper is ready." Anne Michaels appeared in a doorway behind the desk. Seeing Trace, she smiled and said, "Hello, Mr. Burdette."

Trace touched his hat brim. "Miss Michaels." *She has a nice smile.*

"I'll be right there. If you'll excuse me, Mr. Burdette, can't keep Annie's fried chicken waitin'." Michaels pulled a sign from under the counter and set it on the counter. In bold black letters it read: *RING BELL FOR SERVICE.*

Trace nodded and the Michaels' exited to their living quarters. He washed off the day's accumulation of dust. Army habits were hard to break. He had shaved that morning. His clothing was dusty and, taking a brush from his carpetbag, he gave it a thorough brushing. Standing in front of the mirror while he combed his hair, Trace's reflection stared back at him. He was twenty-six years old, and he knew he looked ten years older. His light brown hair had a slight wave. There were fine lines around his blue eyes—eyes that had witnessed more horror than any human had a right to see. Trace shook his head. He had a feeling that the violence and suffering were far from over.

\*   \*   \*

Moonlight streamed through the window beside Anne's bed. A gentle breeze moved the curtains that created shadows on the wall. She had tossed and turned for what seemed like hours, but sleep would not come. Her thoughts were filled with half formed ideas. Should she leave town on a trumped up visit to some relative or stay and face the disgrace that was sure to come?

"Oh, why, Alvin, why did this have to happen to us? Why did you have to die . . ." The tears came, slowly at first, then in a torrent that she could not stop.

Anne knocked on the door of Room 101. "I've brought you some clean towels, Mr. Burdette." There was no answer. She knocked again. No answer. Taking the passkey from the pocket of her apron, Anne unlocked the door and went in. She knew Trace Burdette was an army man, and his room confirmed it. The bed was neatly made, a pair of trousers and a shirt hung on pegs.

His carpetbag was on a chair. A set of brushes and a comb were laid out on the dresser. Anne replaced the soiled towels with clean ones. Of course, he's much older, but I wonder if he's anything like Alvin? Alvin, with the somber expression and responsibility weighing heavy on his shoulders. The pain came then, like a knife in her heart. What am I going to do?

"Poppa, can you watch the desk this afternoon?"

"And what would you want to be doin'?" John placed the gleaming spittoon beside the desk.

Anne struggled to keep her voice steady. "I thought I would take some flowers to Alvin's grave. The bluebonnets are so pretty this year."

John looked at his daughter, his eyes lingering on her pale face. "Are you sure you want to do that?"

"Yes. Don't worry, Poppa. I'll be safe enough."

"Annie, you know there are all sorts of men roamin' around these days. The newspapers are full of reports of violence. Remember what happened in Gilmer to that Negro man, Shack Roberts? He was beaten and left for dead. His former master saved his life, and he lives in Marshall now where the federal troops can protect him. I know you cared a lot for Alvin, but you must think of your own welfare."

"Yes, Poppa, I cared very much for Alvin. I think he was lonely a lot of the time. The least I can do is take some flower to his grave."

John sighed. "Very well, daughter, but please be careful."

"I will, Poppa. I promise."


The small community church stood in the center of the cemetery at the edge of town. Anne had walked the distance and she felt warm and disheveled. The hem of her brown calico dress was dusty. She removed her bonnet and blotted her face. Replacing the bonnet, she moved slowly toward the Burdette family plot. Raw earth with a few weeds on top formed the mound that was Alvin's grave. Anne's hand tightened on the glass jar that held an assortment of wildflowers. This was her first visit since Alvin's death, and all the pain and anxiety surfaced. She knelt and placed the flowers on the grave. Her grief was a living thing that curled around her body, squeezing her heart and tearing at her soul. The tears came, spilling from her eyes and running down her cheeks.

"Why oh why?" Anne did not realize she had said the words aloud.

"Miss Michaels?"

Anne heard the man's voice but her legs refused to move. She raised her head and looked into Trace Burdette's blue eyes now dark with emotion. Without speaking, he held out his hand and helped her to her feet.

"Mr. Burdette, I . . . I." A blush covered her cheeks and she dropped her head.

"It's all right. I understand." He removed his hat and stood looking down at his brother's grave. A myriad of emotions Anne could not read crossed his face. Small headstones marked the graves of his mother, father, brother and sisters. Two girl babies and a boy had died in infancy. Trace's lips moved but Anne could not hear his words. He stepped back and turned to face her.

"Are you all right?" he asked.

"Yes," she murmured. She dabbed at her face with a dainty white handkerchief but kept her gaze focused on the flowers.

"This is the first time I've been here in a long time."

"Your mother and father died during the war, didn't they?"

"Yes. I never saw them again after I left."

"I'm so sorry. I know how hard it was when my mother died. And if I lost Poppa . . ."

Trace donned his hat. "Miss Michaels, it really isn't safe for you to be out here alone. You should permit me to see you home."

"I'm sure you have other things to do, and I don't want to put you to any trouble."

Trace smiled and Anne noticed how it softened his features. "I wouldn't call escorting a pretty girl trouble."

As they walked back to the hotel, Anne wondered if Trace knew a number of people had shunned Alvin because his brother had fought for the North. For some reason, she felt that would not be a new experience for Trace Burdette.

Conversation between them was awkward. Anne could think of nothing to say.

When the couple approached the area where the boardwalk began, Trace tied his horse to the hitch rail in front of the Moore's general store. A man came out of the store carrying a large bundle, partially obscuring his vision. He bumped into Anne who was standing nearby. She lost her balance, grabbed for a post that supported the overhanging roof, but it was too far away. Trace reached her in time to prevent her from falling.

The man dropped the bundle. "I'm awful sorry, ma'am. Are you hurt?"

Anne caught her breath and straightened her bonnet. "No, no, I'm all right."

"I really am sorry, ma'am. I should 'a watched where I was goin'." He glanced at Trace. "Burdette. Heard you was still in town."

"Collins. I didn't know there was a time limit."

"None that I know of. I figure you'll know when it's time to leave." Collins picked up the bundle. He touched his hat brim and nodded to Anne. "Ma'am."

Trace and Anne continued their walk to the hotel. She was flustered and a bit embarrassed.

""Miss Michaels, I hope you're being seen with me doesn't compromise your reputation."

Trace's remark hit home. "No, Mr. Burdettte. I'm not worried about what people may say." *If you only knew.*

*   *   *

The sun was above the horizon when Trace walked into the dog run. He had arrived at the farm the evening before with the supplies he had purchased. After a supper of cold biscuits and tinned peaches, he placed his bedroll in the parlor. There would be time later to look over the loft bedroom he had shared with Alvin.

Uppermost in Trace's mind was the identity of the person or persons camping by the spring. He fed the gelding and decided to take him along. The countryside was full of renegades, and a good piece of horseflesh would be mighty tempting. As he walked across the half-plowed field, Trace thought about the crop he intended to plant. Cotton should bring a good price. It would be difficult to handle the farm by himself. Since he had saved money from his army pay and reenlistment bonus, perhaps he could hire a man to help. There were hundreds of Confederate veterans looking for work, but Trace knew none of them would consider working for a bluebelly, especially a Texas bluebelly. Freed slaves were as plentiful as bluebonnets and might be his only alternative.

When he was into the trees where the horse could not be seen, Trace tied him to a tree limb. He patted the horse's neck and spoke softly. "I'm going to have to give you a name, old boy. Already done some thinkin' on it. Maybe I'll call you *Ulysses.* Don't think the general would be insulted since I believe you got plenty of stayin' power."

The woods was dark and quiet. The creek ran crystal clear as it traveled to its destination. Trace remembered how his mother always ask him or Alvin to fetch spring water when she washed her hair. His features tightened as he thought of how pretty she had been when he was a small boy. Hard work, childbirth and life on the frontier had stolen her beauty.

Her dark hair was streaked with gray and her tanned skin lined when he left to fight for the North.

A soft humming sound interrupted Trace's thoughts. It wasn't singing, exactly, but had a slow rhythm that seemed familiar. Trace stepped off the path and wound his way through the trees. He came out behind the lean to and saw a man bent over the campfire. The odor of something frying whetted Trace's appetite. His breakfast had consisted of the remainder of the biscuits and peaches. The man stood up and turned around. He was not a young man. His gray wooly hair contrasted with his black skin. He stared at Trace and his eyes were wide with fear.

Trace smiled. "Whatever you're cookin' sure smells good."

The man visibly relaxed and grinned, showing several missing teeth. "Yas sur. I'se fryin' some fatback and cornpone. You be welcome to share it."

"Much obliged. By the way, I'm Trace Burdette."

The man's eyes widened and his Adams' apple moved up and down. "Yuse . . . yuse be Massa Alvin's brother?"

"Yes. Did you know my brother?"

"Yas sur. He be a fine young man. I'se mighty sorry he passed." He did not meet Trace's gaze but looked over his shoulder. "My name Moses."

"Pleased to meet you Moses." Trace held out his hand.

Moses hesitated then accepted Trace's gesture of friendship. "Coffee's most chicory but it be hot."

Trace shared Moses' meal and found the simple food tasty. He was curious about how Moses had come to know Alvin, but his instincts told him the old man would not respond favorably to an interrogation. "Appreciate your sharing your meal with me. I brought supplies from town if you need anything."

Moses hesitated before he replied. "Massa Trace, is you gwine be stayin' on this farm?"

"Yes, but you're welcome to remain right here. There's no need for you to leave."

Moses' wrinkled face broke into a grin. "I'se mighty glad to hear that. I been afraid them men's what wear coverin's on their heads and ride around at night might find me and run me off." Moses' grin faded and his expression sobered. "Prob'ly do worse than run me off."

Trace had read in the newspapers about the vigilantes that roamed the land, harassing and robbing the citizens. The Rangers had been disbanded at the close of the war. The Federal Government refused to permit a state to organize bodies of armed men for any purpose. Local officials had little success in keeping the peace, and the state was under military law.

"You're welcome to stay here as long as you like," Trace told Moses.

"If'n them mens finds out, it could cause yo a lot of trouble.'

Trace grinned. "Don't make much difference since I expect plenty of trouble anyway." At the puzzled look on Moses' face, Trace explained. "A Texan who fought for the Union ain't exactly popular in Texas. I plan to put in a crop as soon as I can."

Moses eyes grew round and he stared at Trace. "Massa Alvin was gittin' the field ready when he was . . . was kilt. Maybe you . . . ." Moses turned away and began poking at the campfire.

"What are you trying to say?"

"Ain't tryin' to say nothing 'cept you best watch out fur yo'self."

Trace stored the supplies he had purchased. He would need to cook some victuals but first he wanted to check out the other rooms. The loft where he and Alvin had slept looked much the same as when he left. The crude wooden bedsteads were bare of any coverings and no clothes hung on the pegs on the wall.

Trace suspected the men who wondered the countryside had helped themselves when they discovered the place was not occupied. That would present a problem for him, too. He would have to leave now and then to replenish his supplies, and it was a hard day's ride to town and back. Well, no use to worry about that now.

*       *       *

Trace emerged from the bank and saw Anne coming toward him. He doffed his hat. "Good morning, ma'am."

She offered a hesitant greeting. "Good morning, Mr. Burdette."

Trace caught something in her voice. She was pale and drawn looking. He tried to read the expression on her face. She had taken Alvin's death hard and evidently was still struggling with it.

"How are you?" he asked.

"I . . . I'm fine, sir."

Trace thought he saw moisture form in the corner of her eyes. Something more than his brother's death was bothering the young woman.

25

He looked up and down the boardwalk. There were few people on the street. "It's none of my business, Miss Michaels, but you seem a little distressed this morning."

Anne started to protest, but something in Trace's voice told her he would not believe her. She tried to meet his eyes, but instead lowered her head and stared at her slippers.

He felt a sense of compassion for the young woman who had loved his brother. Perhaps if he walked her home, she would confide in him. "Is your father at the hotel this morning?"

"Yes." She looked at him, a question in her tone.

"I want to have a word with him." Surely, he could think of something to discuss with John Michaels. "May I walk you home?"

"I was going to the bank."

"I'll wait out here for you." He pointed to a nearby bench.

"Thank you. It won't take long." Anne hurried inside.

Anne left the bank and Trace stood. He motioned for her to join him on the bench. Anne hesitated then sat down and spread her skirts between them. Trace did not offer to start a conversation. He wanted to give Anne time to compose her thoughts. Her hands were clasped in her lap, and she twisted a handkerchief into a tight knot. When she looked up at him, Trace saw the raw pain in the depths of her brown eyes. Whatever was wrong, Anne Michaels was frightened to the depths of her soul.

"Please don't think me bold, but since you and Alvin were close to being betrothed, do you want to tell me what's bothering you?"

Anne did not answer and the silence lengthened. Had he offended her? Before he could apologize for his thoughtless remark, she spoke in a voice so low he strained to hear.

"I'm sorry, Mr. Burdette. It's . . . it's very kind of you but it's really not your problem. Nor would it be proper for me to burden you with it."

"You let me worry about that."

Anne swallowed hard and took a deep breath. "If . . . if I were to tell you, I cannot do it here."

Trace felt a sense of relief. He knew Anne must have loved Alvin deeply, and for that reason alone he wanted to help her. "Where would you suggest we meet and when?" He would leave the time and place up to Anne. Her reputation probably was in jeopardy already because she had been seen with him.

Trace mulled over Anne's promise that she would contact him as soon as she could arrange for them to meet. In the meantime, he needed some legal advice. He found Joe Hutcheson in his office.

"Trace," Joe came from around his desk and offered his hand. "How are things going?"

"I'm still trying to get settled in, but I need to get in a crop as soon as I can. That's what I wanted to talk to you about."

"Have a seat and tell me what's on your mind."

Hutcheson motioned to a nearby chair.

"I read about the labor contracts that a land owner can offer the Negroes. What do I need to do if I want to hire a man or two to help me?"

"First, I'll tell you I haven't had much experience with negotiating the contracts. But my interpretation is that you agree on the conditions which have been set, put them in writing and both parties sign them."

"How do I pay them?"

Hutcheson leaned back in his chair and rubbed his chin. "It depends on how you want to handle it. You can hire them for wages or give them a share of the crop. If you pay wages, there are a lot of rules such as to how many hours a day they can work, what you will provide for them such as food, clothing, housing, medical care, etc. You need to work all that out before the papers are drawn up. The Bureau examines the contracts, and charges a fee of one dollar for each employer and twenty-five cents for each freedman. If you want me to, I'll check into the procedures to make sure I have the correct information."

"I'd appreciate that. While you're doing that maybe I can line up some prospects. How about your fee?" Trace grinned and added, "That is if you don't mind accepting Yankee money."

Joe laughed. "It's the best kind these days. Let's just wait until we finish our business before I send you a bill."

"Fair enough," Trace answered as he shook the lawyer's hand.

# CHAPTER FOUR

T HE SUN WAS PEEPING OVER the horizon when Trace walked into the field where Alvin died. A scraggly crop of weeds covered the plowed earth. He needed to get the cottonseed in the ground as soon as possible. With Ulysses trailing behind, Trace headed for Moses' camp to enlist his help. Trace's intuition told him the old man would be hard to convince that labor contracts were necessary. Surely, the old man knew young men who would be interested in working for wages.

Trace found Moses hunched over the campfire, stirring something in a skillet. He looked up, a grin creasing his wrinkled features. As he started to rise, Trace waved the old man to remain at his task.

""Mornin', Massa Trace. Yo had breakfast yit?"

"Yes, but I'll take a cup of your coffee." Trace had developed a taste for the old man's brew.

Moses filled a cup and handed it to Trace. "I's makin' rabbit gravy. I sure am obliged to you for the flour and other fixin's you give me."

"Glad I could help out." Trace took a sip of the scalding liquid. The flavor was even better since Moses had added more coffee to the chicory. Trace sat down on a nearby stump and contemplated how to approach Moses about the labor contracts. Best to get right to the point. He fortified himself with another swallow of coffee.

"Moses, I don't mean to pry into your private life, but I was wondering if you have any kinfolk living nearby?"

Moses shook his head, his wrinkled features reflecting a deep sadness. "No, suh. My woman, she died of the fever long time ago. One of my boys done run off to Californie and the other was killed by a Rebel soldier."

"I'm sorry, Moses. I know how it feels to lose kinfolk."

"I does have grandsons, two of them. Names Rufus and Jimbo. I don't exactly know where they is. I ain't seen them for awhile."

"Do you think you might be able to find them?" Trace asked.

"Guess I could ask around. Why you want them, Massa Trace?"

Trace finished the last of his coffee and stood up. "I'm going to need some help putting in the crops and I'm hoping to hire a couple of men. I'll pay a fair wage, but there's a law about signing contracts with everything spelled out."

Moses eyes widened and his brow wrinkled. "What you mean, wages, contracts? I don't know nothing about that law stuff."

"You will be paid plus certain other benefits like number of hours to work, medical care, housing allowance and more.

"I kin try to find them boys. Don't know what they say. Seein' as how you fought with them Yankees, they might be willin'."

Trace grinned, but there was no humor in his voice when he answered. "That's not likely to be a popular decision, but we'll handle that problem when the time comes."

*       *       *

A week passed and Trace had not heard from Joe nor had Moses been able to find his grandsons. The weeds had been chopped from the field and the plowing started. Ulysses put up such a fuss when harnessed to the plow that Trace decided it would save time if he purchased a team already broken to the plow. He would need them to pull the wagon he intended to buy at a later date.

As he ground beans for coffee, Trace calculated there were enough left for a pot or two. The larder was running low since he had given Moses a generous amount of supplies. He thought of Anne Michaels and wondered if she still wanted to talk with him. It seemed a trip to town was warranted.

Riding past the cemetery, Trace thought of his family. He and Alvin had shared their chores, played together and managed to get into mischief without too much difficulty. Their father, a stern man when the need arose, did not discourage his sons from book learning and the semblance of good manners their mother tried to teach them. The bittersweet memories brought to mind that Alvin did not have a grave marker. He should attend to that chore right away. His thoughts running full circle, he wondered if Anne Michaels would like to help him choose a stone.

Trace found Anne behind the desk at the hotel. Her yellow gown emphasized her pale skin. "Good morning, ma'am."

"Good morning, Mr. Burdette."

"Miss Michaels, I don't want to cause you any more pain, but I was wondering if you would like to help me chose a stone for Alvin's grave?"

The faint traces of color in Anne's face faded to leave her complexion chalky white. She swallowed hard and stared at Trace.

"That is of course, if your father has no objections."

Anne swallowed again and spoke in a soft voice. "He's upstairs repairing a window in one of the rooms. But, I'm sure he would not object. If you'll be seated, I'll ask him." Anne avoided looking directly at Trace. "I'll need a moment to freshen up."

"There's no rush. Take your time. It's too hot to walk out there and back. I'll hire a rig at the livery."

Anne was waiting when Trace returned with the rig. She had exchanged the yellow frock for one of navy blue and wore a straw bonnet with dark blue streamers. She looked composed, but Trace noticed the tight lines around her mouth. She was silent on the ride to the cemetery, and Trace did not try to make conversation. After all, what could he say to the young woman whose grief seemed to surpass his own?

The cemetery was deserted, the sun shining brightly on the headstones. Trace guided the horse to a stand of trees near the fence. He assisted Anne from the buggy. Her hand tightened in his, and he was surprised at the strength in her grip.

"I'm sorry I couldn't bring flowers but they are not very pretty now." Anne, holding her skirt up, kept her eyes focused on the ground. She seemed reluctant to let go of Trace's hand as he guided her toward the Burdette plot.

Trace nodded but did not speak. Alvin's grave had been leveled off and new grass was beginning to choke out the weeds. No doubt, the families of the Confederate soldiers buried there were responsible for the well-tended graves. He was grateful they had considered Alvin one of their own despite the fact that his brother was a traitor. Anne stumbled and stopped short of Alvin's gravesite.

Trace placed his arm around her. "I'm sorry, Miss Michaels, this was not a good idea. Let me take you home."

"It is not . . . not that I have not accepted Alvin's death. I know he is gone and I can do nothing about it." The tears came then, sliding down her checks as she struggled to control them.

"Let's go back to the buggy, out of the sun." Trace managed to turn the girl back and helped her up onto the seat. He sat down beside her but made no effort to take up the lines, or to talk. Anne looked at him, her eyes bright with tears. She shook her head in a slow helpless motion.

Trace broke the silence. "Miss Michaels, won't you tell me what is upsetting you so. I don't know if I can help, but I will certainly try."

Anne looked down at her hands, which were tightly clenched, in her lap. "I . . . I . . . I need to talk to someone but . . . but . . . there isn't anybody I can go to."

Trace reached out and stroked her hands. "You can tell me, you know. I'm a good listener."

"It's very hard for me, Mr. Burdette. Especially since you are Alvin's brother and . . . . Besides, what will you think of me when you learn the truth? What will everybody think of me?"

"I'm sure you're a fine young woman, Miss Michaels, and whatever it is you want to tell me won't change that."

"I can't hold on much longer, anyway. I would rather you knew before the rest of the town does."

"What is it?" Trace continued to pat her hands.

"You already know that Alvin and I were . . . well, interested in one another. It went further than that, Mr. Burdette. We were secretly engaged. Alvin wanted to wait until he had a good crop before we announced our plans. We hoped to marry in the fall, after the harvest." Anne took a deep breath and turned her head away. Her voice barely above a whisper, she said, "I'm going to have Alvin's baby."

Trace was stunned by Anne's revelation. He had never considered that might be the problem. No wonder she appeared distraught. Trace could well imagine the impact the vicious gossip would have on the frail young woman.

"Does your father know?" Trace asked the first question that came to his mind.

"Oh, no! It would kill him. I must try to find a way to keep it from him and have mentioned I would like to visit my aunt in San Antonio.

"Poppa thinks the trip would be good for me. She is a wonderful woman and will not turn me away."

"But what about afterward? When the baby is born? What will you do then?"

"I don't know. Perhaps my aunt and I can think of something."

"I know this is painful for you, but when is the baby due?"

Anne hesitated. "Some time in September, I think."

"My God, Anne, haven't you been to a doctor?"

The color rose in her face and she turned away. "No, I cannot see Dr. Goodrich. He . . . he asked to call on me when he first came back from the war. I refused him because Alvin and I . . . ." Anne fumbled with the strings on her reticule.

"There must be other doctors nearby."

"Yes, there is Dr. Parker here and a Dr. Dickinson in Navasota. But how could I go there without telling my father?"

Trace stroked his chin, his thoughts racing. He wanted to help Anne, not only for Alvin's sake, but because he liked the young woman.

"I have an idea that might work. Let's say that I ask your father if I may call on you. I don't think he'll object. I can escort you to church, any social function that might be coming up. Something like that. Then after a week or so, we can go for a buggy ride. I'll take you to Navasota to see a doctor."

Anne was silent for a moment. When she spoke, her voice held a bitter note. "I appreciate your offer, Mr. Burdette, but I can't see how it will help. No, I must go away before it's too late and the whole town knows."

"The doctor's visit is necessary for your health, ma'am. As for the rest of it, let's give it a little more time."

"Time is something I don't have, Mr. Burdette."

"Promise you won't leave until you see the doctor in Navasota. That shouldn't be over a week or so."

"All right, a week then."

Trace cupped Anne's face in his hand and smiled at her. "Try not to worry. Everything is going to work out."

John Michaels was behind the desk when Trace and Anne returned to the hotel. Anne excused herself and left the two men alone.

"How are things going at your farm?" John asked.

"Not as well as I would like. I have a field ready for planting but could use some help. Don't suppose you know of anybody wanting work?"

John hesitated before replying. Then, his tone apologetic, answered, "There's plenty of men lookin' for work but . . . ."

Trace's features hardened. "Yeah, I know. They won't work for a traitor to The Cause."

"Wished things wasn't that way. This country needs to pull together so people can get back on their feet."

"You're right about that," Trace answered. "I don't know if I should bring this up now, but I see no reason to wait. Mr. Michaels, Miss Anne is a mighty fine young woman, and I would like your permission to call on her."

John's expression did not reflect the surprise Trace had expected. "I been expecting something like this or maybe I was just hoping it would happen. No disrespect to Alvin, he was a fine young man. But he *was* young and I think my Anne needs an older man that understands the responsibility of taking on a wife."

"I mentioned to Miss Anne that I would be asking you and she had no objections. The only problem I have is that I don't want to compromise her reputation by being seen in my company."

John came from around the desk. "Don't you worry 'bout that. A person should live by his own conscience, not by what other people think is right. There's plenty in Grimes County that don't want their doin's made public."

Trace nodded. "I think I know what you're referring to and I agree with you. If you have a beef about something, bring it out in the open."

"That's what a man should do, but it's safer for them to keep things covered up."

\*     \*     \*

"I've already asked Miss Anne if I may escort her to church next Sunday. That is, with your permission, of course."

"You have that, my boy!"

Trace and Anne caused quite a stir when they entered the Methodist Church on Sunday morning. Both could hear the whispered comments and make out some of the words: traitor, respectable, reputation; all rang inside Anne's head. Trace's grip on her arm tightened and she looked at him out of the corner of her eye. His mouth, set in stern lines, and narrowed eyes gave no quarter. Adjusting herself in the pew, Anne stared straight ahead. The minister saw her and smiled as he approached the pulpit.

"I am going to deviate from my prepared sermon today," the minister said. "There is so much unrest and ill will among us that I think it needs addressing. You all know the Lord's commandment, 'Love they neighbor as thyself.'"

Anne kept her eyes focused on the Reverend, but her ears were tuned to the murmurs from the worshippers around her. Even if she left Anderson, she knew that time would tell a story that the women would put together. The couple left the church before the majority of the congregation was on its feet. Trace exchanged looks with the preacher and he nodded his understanding.

Trace was silent as he guided the horse toward the hotel. He had invited John to take the noon meal with them at the Fanthrop Inn, but John declined, saying he was going fishing with a friend.

When they were seated in the buggy, Anne broke the silence. "I'm sorry, Mr. Burdette, but I don't think I'm up to a meal right now."

"I understand. I know it's difficult for you. I have something I want to talk with you about. Do you have any objections if we go for a ride out of town?"

"No. In fact it would be nice to get away for awhile."

"Have you ever been to the farm?"

Anne smiled, the sadness in her voice coming through. "Yes, Alvin took me there once so that I could see where we would be living."

"Let's just go in that direction. We can turn back whenever you want."

Trace was lost in thought and there was little conversation. He had done some heavy thinking about Anne's situation as well as his own. Both of them would be outcasts in the long run. That did not bother him. He expected as much when he returned to Texas. Alvin was dead and could not be hurt by idle tongues. However, Anne was another matter. The young woman and her child would face a lifetime of shame and disgrace.

The farm came into view and Trace realized neither of them had spoken a word. He helped Anne from the buggy and guided her toward the dogtrot.

Trace grinned as he waved toward the house. "I don't know if you want to go inside or not. I'm afraid I'm a typical bachelor when it comes to housekeeping."

"This will be fine," Anne responded as she sat down in the old rocker that had been Trace's mother's. She spread out her skirts and leaned back. "It's very peaceful here."

"I think we could both use a drink of cold water. I'll fetch a bucket from the well."

The water was sweet and cold. "I could probably rustle us up something to eat," Trace offered.

"Thank you, but I'm really not hungry."

"If you're sure?"

"I'm sure."

"Then, I'd like to discuss an idea with you."

"You know I'm willing to listen to whatever you have to say."

"Well this is kind 'a hard to put into words but I'll do the best I can. Miss Anne, there's no denying you need help with your . . . situation. I know you don't really want to leave your father and go to your aunt and, even if you did, you would have to decide what to do after . . . after the baby is born. If you come back to Anderson, it will be just as hard as if you stayed here to begin with."

"I know that, Mr. Burdette, but I don't know what else to do. I guess I could stay on with my aunt, but . . ."

"I know you and Alvin would have married if he had lived. He left the farm to me, and I intend to stay on it. It won't be an easy life and I can't promise you much, but I can give you and the baby a home."

Anne's eyes opened wide and she gasped. "Mr. Burdette, I . . . I don't know what to say except that if I were to live here with you the situation would become intolerable. Besides, my father would never allow me to do such a thing."

Trace took both her hands in his. "I told you I wasn't very good at this sort of thing. What I'm trying to say is, Miss Anne, will you marry me?"

Anne stared at Trace, her eyes wide, her mouth open, trying to speak. He sat down beside her, her hand still in his. "I know every woman dreams of a fairy tale courtship and wedding. I'm far from a knight in shining armor, but I will do my best by you. Your child will be a Burdette which is no more than right."

Anne struggled to find the words but they would not come. She had loved Alvin with all her heart and to marry his brother somehow seemed to betray his memory. "I . . . I don't know what to say. I . . . ," she could not go on.

"I know you loved Alvin, and I don't expect you to feel that way toward me. I do not expect to you to be my wife in the . . . the . . . biblical sense. I just want to protect you and my brother's child."

Tears formed in Anne's eyes and trickled down her face. "You would do that for me?"

"It's as much for myself as for you. I'm protecting Alvin's good name, too. Do you want to think about it for a few days and then give me your answer?"

Anne shook her head. "No, I don't need to think about it. I will marry you, Mr. Burdette."

# CHAPTER FIVE

TRACE, ANNE AND JOHN WERE seated in the family quarters of the hotel. Trace had convinced Anne that they should speak with her father at once. She was nervous, her hands twisting a dainty handkerchief into knots.

"Mr. Michaels, I know Anne and I haven't known each other very long, but sometimes it doesn't take long for a man to know when he has found a woman he wants for his wife."

John's eyebrows flew upward. "Marriage?" he croaked. Turning to Anne, his mouth moved but no sound emerged. After several attempts, he managed to speak, "Daughter, are you sure you know what you are doing? It has only been a couple of months since Alvin's death. Are you not possibly confusing the two men? No doubt Trace here is a good man, but he is not Alvin."

"No, Poppa, Trace is not Alvin, nor would I want him to be. He has been very kind to me and I appreciate that. His . . . situation is not easy, and he needs a wife who will stand beside him when trouble comes. And there will be trouble, Poppa, you know that."

John nodded. "Yes, there will be trouble, but to marry so quickly is . . . You two should take time to get to know each other."

Anne's face flamed and she dropped her head. Her voice barely audible, she answered. "I'm sorry, Poppa, so sorry. But we can't wait. I'm going to have Alvin's baby."

John's face paled and this time he could not find his voice.

"Mr. Michaels, I know Anne and Alvin loved each other and would have married had he lived. He would not want to see her disgraced, and I don't want to see his good name sullied. I want to protect Anne and Alvin both. I promise I will be a good husband and the child will be Anne's and mine and will carry the Burdette name."

\*    \*    \*

The wedding ceremony was quietly arranged. The minister of the Methodist Church was reluctant to perform the ceremony until he realized the young couple were determined to wed. Trace and Anne exchanged vows in the Reverend Foster's parlor with Mrs. Foster and John as witnesses. Anne's voice was soft but steady and Trace admired her composure. She wore a pale blue gown with a white lace collar. He placed the plain gold band on her finger, and the minister pronounced them husband and wife. Their lips touched briefly in a chaste kiss.

John insisted on going back to the hotel for a meal, which Anne had prepared that morning. The situation was awkward and the newlyweds were soon on their way to the farm. Trace had purchased a wagon and team, and Anne's trunk and other belongings occupied the space behind the seat. Trace picked up supplies before the wedding in order to save Anne from possible embarrassment. Word of their hasty marriage would be public knowledge soon enough. The town gossips took great delight in spreading their *news* to anyone who would listen.

There was little conversation between the couple as they traveled. Trace knew he needed to say something to Anne about the physical side of their marriage. No doubt, the young woman was frightened and did not know what to expect. Her relationship with Alvin had been a brief one that hardly prepared her for the marriage bed.

Trace guided the wagon to a shady spot beside the road. "Let's stop and rest a bit." He helped Anne down and took a canteen from the wagon bed. Trace felt her fingers tremble when he handed her the canteen. She took several dainty sips of water.

Before he could change his mind, he spoke. "Anne, we haven't had much chance to talk about . . . about the physical side of our marriage. I want you to know that I do not expect to share your bed. I'm settled in my old room. I'll put your things in the room that belonged to my Ma and Pa. You can fix it up any way you want to."

"Anne's face colored and she looked down at her feet. "I don't know what to say."

"No need to say anything." He stepped closer and put his arm around her shoulder. "Don't worry. Things are going to work out just fine."

They reached the farm an hour later, and Trace swung Anne from the wagon seat. She looked around and he saw a tear form in the corner of her eye. No doubt she was thinking of the time when she would have arrived as Alvin's bride.

Forcing a gaiety he did not feel, Trace took her hand. "Every new bride deserves to be carried over the threshold." Before she could protest, he scooped her into his arms and headed for the house.

\*    \*    \*

In the days following their marriage, Trace and Anne settled into a routine. Trace was up early, built a fire in the big black range and brought fresh water from the well. The first few days Anne rose and prepared their breakfast. The bouts of morning sickness struck without warning. Trace had no experience with pregnancy but he urged her to stay in bed. He made sure the chamber pot was handy, brought cold cloths to place on her forehead and tried to make her comfortable.

One afternoon when Anne felt well enough to be left alone, he went in search of Moses. Trace was behind in getting his crop in, and he needed to find help as soon as possible. He found Moses at his camp with a young man. *I hope that is his* grandson *and he's willing to work for me.*

"Massa Trace, is you alright? You ain't been 'round for awhile." Moses said, his voice filled with concern.

"Yes, I'm fine. I've been busy getting my new wife settled in." Trace watched the expression on Moses face turn to one of amazement.

"Yo all done got married?"

"Yes. Her name is Anne. Her father owns a hotel in Anderson."

Moses stared at Trace, his eyes wide. "Yo done married Miss Anne, Mr. Alvin's intended?"

It was Trace's turn to be surprised. "You know about Alvin and Anne?"

"Yas sir. Mr. Alvin tol' me he was goin' to marry Miss Anne as soon as he saved up some money."

The young man spoke before Trace could think of a suitable reply. "Granpappy say yo needs hep with yo crop." He was thin and wiry looking, his head covered with tight black curls. "My name be Rufus. I be willin' to hep you some."

"Good to meet you, Rufus." Trace offered his hand.

The man's eyes widened and he looked at Trace with disbelief written on his face. Trace waited. Rufus grasped Trace's outstretched hand. His grip was hesitant at first, but then he grinned, showing gleaming white teeth. "Yas sah, I make you a good hand, sah. Granpappy say we have to put our mark on some paper sayin' we work for wages."

"That's about the size of it, but the papers haven't been made out yet. I'll tell you what I know about them, and we can talk about wages. The lawyer in Anderson will take care of it for us."

When Trace returned from talking with Moses, he found Anne in the kitchen in the midst of preparing supper. Her hair was tied back with a yellow ribbon and she wore a white apron over a gray calico dress. Her cheeks were flushed from the heat of the range. *How young and pretty she looks.* He had no regrets about marrying her and raising his brother's child.

"Are you sure you are up to this?" he asked, surveying the bowls and pans on the table.

She gave him a shy smile and answered, "Oh, yes, I feel fine. There was a piece of ham, some potatoes and onions in the larder, and I'm making potato soup. It is too late to make bread, but I will bake some biscuits. There isn't any butter, but I found a jar of honey."

Trace grinned. "Sounds like a feast to me. Is there anything I can do to help you?"

"No, but thank you for offering. It will be a little while before it's ready."

"In that case, I think I'll feed the horses. Ulysses needs a good currying too."

"You're a good cook, Anne. This is mighty fine fare."

Anne smiled and Trace could see the compliment pleased her. "I'm glad you like it. My mother taught me to cook when I was a little girl."

"She was a good teacher," Trace said as he reached for another biscuit.

Anne filled Trace's coffee cup, but declined the beverage herself. "I'm not very fond of coffee," she told him.

Trace eyed her thoughtfully. "I'm sorry. I should have thought to buy tea for you."

"That's all right. I brought a tin with me but haven't felt like making it."

"Why didn't you tell me? I don't know much about fixing it but I can learn."

Anne's eyes grew misty and she turned her head. Trace rose from the table and came to her side. He knelt and cupped his hand beneath her chin. Looking into her eyes, he struggled for the words to convey his feelings. "Please don't cry, Anne. I know this can't be easy for you. I'm not used to being around women. I hope you will help me polish off the rough edges."

Anne smiled and shook her head. "You don't have any rough edges, Trace Burdette. You are the kindest man I've ever known."

It was Trace's turn to look embarrassed. He sat down and picked up his coffee cup. After a few minutes of silence, he decided to tell her what was on his mind. "I've been thinking we need a cow and a few chickens. I can probably get them from a farm around here."

"I will be glad to take care of them, but I'm afraid you will have to teach me."

"That's another thing I want to talk about. Since you have never lived on a farm and considering your . . . your health, I think you should have somebody, another woman, to help you with the chores."

Anne's eyes widened in surprise. "Oh, Trace, I'm stronger than I look. There's no need for you to have that added expense."

Trace hesitated. *Might as well come out with it.* "Don't worry about that. There's another reason I want you to have somebody around, especially when I'm not here. There are a lot of men roaming around these parts, and most of them are up to no good. I would feel a lot better if you were not here alone."

Anne's face paled, but she remained composed. Trace knew she was concerned.

"Did Alvin ever mention an old Negro man named Moses?"

A smile brightened her face. "Oh, yes, I met Moses when Alvin brought me to the farm."

"I'm glad to hear that. Moses is still here and he keeps an eye out even though you don't see him. His grandson, Rufus, has agreed to help me put in the crops. If I can find a woman to help you, that should let people know the place is plenty occupied."

41

The next morning after breakfast, Trace set out for a neighboring farm. The Arnold place was several miles to the west of Anderson. There had been no hostility between the two families until the outbreak of the war. The Arnolds had owned slaves and when Trace's political views were made known, the Arnolds were among the first families to break the bonds of friendship.

*If I wait to find people who have forgotten the past, I'll never find anybody. Best to take them one at a time. Surely, some of these people will be broadminded enough to do business with me. At any rate, money talks and they need money.*

The Arnold farm showed the effects of the war. The once well-tended fields were spotty with weeds although a crop had been planted. Trace's memory took him back to the time when the Negroes hoed in the fields, their voices raised in song. At the time, Trace wondered how they could sound happy being in bondage as they were.

By the time he reached the main house, a man stood on the porch, a rifle cradled in his arms. Trace guided Ulysses to the hitch rail. "Howdy," Trace offered.

The man stepped off the porch and Trace recognized him as the youngest Arnold son. The man did not invite Trace to dismount as was the custom. His eyes narrowed and he shifted a wad of tobacco from one cheek to the other.

"You are Trace Burdette, ain't you?" he asked, his voice harsh.

"Yes. You were a boy when I left."

"Yeah, me and Alvin was good friends. Still was up until he got hisself killed."

Trace's heart skipped a beat. "Got himself killed?" Trace's voice held an edge. "I was told it was an accident."

Arnold spat a gob of tobacco juice at a large beetle, pinning the insect to the ground. "Yeah, guess it was. I heard you was back but didn't think you would stay around here."

Trace shifted in the saddle. "The farm is mine and I plan to work it. Reason I'm here is to see if you have a cow and some chickens to sell?"

Arnold let out a guffaw. "Well, don't that beat all. A turncoat wantin' to do business with a Reb. Nawh, I ain't got nothing to sell you, Burdette. And I doubt any of the other farmers do either."

Trace could feel the heat climb up the back of his neck. With supreme effort, he held his temper in check. With a long level look at Arnold, he turned Ulysses toward the road.

Out of sight of the Arnold farm, Trace guided Ulysses off the road to the shade of a live oak tree. His gut was knotted in anger. He had expected the reception he got but it still galled him. Pulling the *makin's* from his shirt pocket, he built a smoke. Trace drew the smoke deep into his lungs, held it there a moment, then exhaled. The anger slowly subsided. The luxury of giving in to his feelings was one he could not afford.

If memory served him right, a family by the name of Moore owned a farm to the south. Trace reined Ulysses onto the trail. He surveyed the countryside. The fields he remembered being tilled by Negro slaves now lay choked with weeds. An uneasy feeling began to surround him. When he reached the lane leading to the Moore farm, he saw the signs of neglect. The buildings were ramshackle and rusted farm implements lay strewn about.

"Hello, the house," Trace called, the sound of his voice echoing in the stillness.

There was no sign of life anywhere. Wonder why the carpetbaggers haven't taken over this place? They seem to have a hold everywhere. Trace looked toward the sun. No use wasting time here. There might be time to check out one more farm before he headed home.

"Hold it right there!" A man stepped from the brush carrying a rifle pointed in Trace's direction.

Trace brought Ulysses to a halt and eyed the man. He was of medium height. A heavy beard covered most of his face and his hair hung long beneath a battered hat. *He must be one of the Jackson's.* Trace's face betrayed no emotion as he met the man's cold stare.

"Heard you was back, Burdette. What's a traitor like you doin' on Jackson land?"

Trace felt the hair at the back of his neck prickle. That usually meant someone was behind him, but he gave no sign of being aware of it. "I'm interested in buying a milk cow and some chickens. Thought you might have some for sale."

The man's shocked look was replaced with a malicious gleam in his dark eyes. He turned his attention to the side of the trail as a man came hobbling out of the brush. He walked with a crutch under one arm, and Trace saw that his right leg was off above the knee. The revolver in his hand was pointed at Trace's chest.

"Remember me Burdette?" the crippled man asked.

Trace had no difficulty recognizing Job Jackson. He had been a hot head when he was young, and the two had exchanged fisticuffs on more than one occasion. The other man must be Isaac, the older brother. Both men had left Texas to join Hood's Brigade before Trace went north. Isaac moved closer and Job followed. His gait was awkward but the pistol in his hand never wavered. Before Trace could respond, Job spoke again.

"You know, Burdette, it could 'a been your bullet that cost me my leg." Job's voice was soft, but his narrow features were tight with anger.

"Most likely was and if it wasn't, it don't matter much. He killed and wounded his share of our men." Isaac did not attempt to keep the bitterness from his voice. His dark eyes burned with the desire to even the score.

"The war is over, Jackson. It would be better for all of us if we put it in the past where it belongs." Trace was careful to keep his hands still and in plain sight. One wrong move would set the men off.

"The war will never be over! Not until the damn Yankees are drove out of Texas. That includes you and your kind."

Trace felt the anger burn in his throat and make its way to his gut. If he was going to survive in this hostile land that he had once called home and hoped to again, he had to find a solid middle ground. "I'm sorry you feel that way, Jackson. I don't like the carpetbaggers any more than you do, but they are bringing in money that Texas needs to get back on her feet."

"Us *Texans* don't need Yankee blood money. And speakin' of money . . . ."

Before Trace could respond, Isaac poked the rifle in his midsection. "You carryin' any of that Yankee gold on you?"

Trace drew in a breath and his body stiffened. He was not the young boy that Job had traded blows with, coming out the winner most of the time. Trace had learned to defend himself by men who fought in the streets and back alleys of New York City and the wharfs of Boston. "I'm not looking for a fight, but I won't run from one either."

Isaac pulled the rifle away and stepped back. With a low bow, he invited Trace to dismount. All his concentration centered on Isaac, Trace did not see Job as he positioned himself behind Trace. As the two men squared off, Trace turned his head in time to see Job raise his crutch to strike. With Isaac in front of him and Job at his back, Trace hesitated a split second too long. His head exploded in a burst of pain.

# CHAPTER SIX

"**M**z. Anne! Mz. Anne! Come quick."
Anne heard the call and hurried out to the dogtrot. Moses and a his grandson were carrying a body toward her.

Anne recognized her husband's limp form. "Oh, my God! What happened?"

"Don' know, Mz. Anne. Dog, he come into camp carryin' on sumpun awful. We follered him and found Massa Trace tied to his horse 'bout a half mile away. Now, don' you swoon. He still alive and he need doctorin'."

Anne swallowed hard and steeled herself to what lay ahead. "Please bring him into the house." She led the way to her bedroom.

"He be all bloody, ma'am." Moses told her.

"That doesn't matter." She stripped off the patchwork quilt, and Moses and Rufus laid Trace face down on the bed. Anne felt the gorge rise in her throat when she saw the wound on the back of his head. *I can't breakdown now. Trace needs me.*

"I'm going to fetch a pan of water and some cloths. While I'm gone, do you think you could get him undressed?"

"Yesum." Moses knelt to remove Trace's boots.

When she returned to the bedroom, Trace was stripped with the sheet covering his lower body. Anne, who had never seen her husband undressed, thought how different he looked lying silent and unmoving from the strong competent man she married. His hair was matted with blood and there were bruises on his arms and shoulders. She tore the cloth into bandages and washed off most of the bloodstains. Making a compress, she placed it on the head wound. Trace moaned but did not regain consciousness.

"I'm going send for the doctor. Can one of you go into town? Go to the hotel and tell my father about this. He will fetch the doctor."

"I be glad to go," the young man offered.

"Mz. Anne, this be Rufus, my grandson. He come to he'p Massa Trace with the plantin'."

"I'm pleased to meet you, Rufus. I have some cornbread left over from dinner if you would like to eat a bite before you leave."

"Thank you, ma'am. I jist take a piece or two and eat it on my way to town. Massa Trace need hep real bad."

While Moses sat with Trace, Anne busied herself with making fresh coffee. She refilled the pot with water so it would be hot when the doctor arrived, wiped the tabletop and set out clean cups and spoons.

Although she knew the doctor had not had time to reach the farm, she glanced out the window as if to will him to appear. *Please hurry.* Her mind was filled with thoughts of how kind Trace had been to her. To think the man had given up any hope he might have had for marriage with a woman he loved, brought tears to her eyes.

Anne forced her thoughts to more practical matters. Perhaps Moses was hungry. Taking a skillet from its hook above the hearth, she set it on the range. Thank goodness, she had sliced the bacon that morning; otherwise, she would probably cut off her fingers. She placed the slices in the skillet and turned to get a fork from the cupboard drawer.

"Mz Anne," Moses poked his head around the kitchen door. "I doesn't mean to skeer you, but Massa Trace, he be restless. He mutterin' somethin' 'bout them Jacksons. Don't make no sense to me."

Anne took the skillet off the stove and set it aside. Wiping her hands on her apron, she followed Moses into the bedroom. Trace had thrown the covers off and was thrashing around. Moses quickly covered his lower body. Anne motioned for Moses to go to the other side of the bed. She laid her hand on Trace's arm. "Trace, it's Anne. Can you hear me?" His words were unintelligible, but he quieted . . .

"Moses, let's see if we can turn him on his side. It will take the pressure off the wound." The two of them managed to accomplish the task. Anne bent to straighten the covers when Trace opened his eyes. He stared at her. "Anne." His voice was barely above a whisper.

"Yes, Trace. I'm here. Moses and Rufus found you on the side of the road and brought you home. I've sent for the doctor."

Trace opened his mouth to speak, but Anne shook her head. "Don't try to talk. Save your strength. The doctor should be here soon."

Dr. Parker arrived accompanied by John Michaels. The doctor was nearing forty and his dark hair and beard were liberally sprinkled with gray.

"Oh, Poppa, I'm so glad you came." Anne ran into her father's outstretched arms.

John held Anne and gently patted her back.

"Doc will patch Trace up. Everything is going to be all right."

Rufus saw to the animals while the doctor examined his patient. "You can tell us what happened later, Mr. Burdette. You've had a nasty blow to the head, and I must get the wound cleaned and apply medication." Grateful for the hot water Anne provided, the doctor worked quickly and Trace soon had a large bandage on the back of his head.

Anne's face colored when the doctor suggested she wash the bruises with a mixture of warm water and baking soda. Trace's expression conveyed some kind of emotion and he started to get out of bed.

The doctor held out a restraining hand. "Oh, no, Mr. Burdette, you need to stay in bed for a few days. Head wounds are tricky. You're going to have one giant headache for a while, probably a few dizzy spells, and your vision might not clear up right away. I'll leave some laudanum with Mrs. Burdette." He turned to Anne. "If you will bring me a cup of water, I'll administer the first dose myself."

"Doc," Trace croaked his voice raspy, "I'm not staying in this bed. The Jackson brothers stole my money, and my rifle. I aim to get them back."

"Let the authorities handle it. I will report the incident to the sheriff myself when I return to town. You need to concentrate on recovering from your wound."

"The law won't do anything, Doc. Not for me, anyway."

The bitterness in Trace's voice was not lost on the doctor. "I was a surgeon during the war, and I don't have to tell you what that was like. In order to remain a doctor, I had to put the past behind me. It's over and we need to move forward. Holding on to it will only cause more pain and suffering."

"That don't mean a man has to sit back and let a bunch of . . . of soreheads steal from him. The money can't be identified, but the rifle can. A '67 Henry repeater is a weapon most civilians couldn't afford even if it was available. The army bought the first guns that were made. That one was given to me by my commanding officer when I left the army."

After his initial greeting to his daughter, John had remained silent. Now he stepped closer to the bedside. "I know how you feel, Trace, but Doc is right. You need to heal up first."

Anne handed the cup of water to the doctor who dosed it with a generous amount of laudanum. "Drink this," he commanded. Trace recognized an order when he heard one and emptied the cup.

Anne stood in the doorway. "Doctor, I've made fresh coffee if you would like some before you return to town."

"That would be most welcome, Mrs. Burdette," he answered. "Then I will give you instructions concerning your husband's care."

The term *your husband* still caused Anne some discomfort. Their marriage had not been consummated and she knew it would not be, at least not until her child was born. She forced her thoughts to concentrate on the baby. Since the doctor was there, it would be a good time to talk with him about her condition.

Before she could arrange a talk with the doctor, John spoke. "Annie, we have a new guest at the hotel. A Miss Regina Mills. She is from the North and has come here to teach the Negroes."

"I heard about her arrival," Dr. Barnes said. He grinned. "I hear she is very pretty, too."

"She is Doc. Right pretty. I hope you get to meet her soon, Annie. She is a nice young lady, and I know you will like her."

Anne smiled at her father. She knew he was concerned about her lack of female friends. Perhaps a stranger, even if she was a Yankee, would be less critical of her marriage. "That would be nice, Poppa. Maybe you could bring her for a visit soon."

"That sounds like a good idea. I have already told her about you. Doc will be coming back in a few days to check on Trace, and you could send her an invitation then."

John and the doctor left soon afterwards. Anne did not have an opportunity to talk with the physician.

Shadows crept along the wall as the purple twilight faded to gray and darkness descended on the land. Anne lighted the lamp in the bedroom. Trace was sleeping, the laudanum keeping him quiet and still. She gazed into his face. The fine lines around his eyes were smoothed out and his stern jaw relaxed. *He has seen his share of hard times. It's not right that a man should have to pay such a heavy price to defend his beliefs.* But, Anne knew there were still many trials ahead and vowed she would stand by Trace no matter what happened.

The laudanum kept Trace quiet most of the night. Anne managed to nap on the sofa in the parlor. Moses and Rufus disappeared into the night after telling her they would keep watch nearby.

"Anne," Trace called just as dawn was breaking.

Anne came wake with a start, disoriented from sleeping in a strange bed. She sat up, her joints aching. The horsehair was rough although she had padded it with a heavy comforter.

"Anne," Trace called again. His voice held a note of fear.

"I'll be right there." She straightened her wrinkled clothing and patted her hair into a semblance of order.

Trace was sitting up in bed, looking as if he were about to get up. "Trace! You are supposed to stay in bed and lie still. The doctor was very specific about that. A head injury is a serious matter."

"I don't care what that sawbones said. I need to . . . to relieve myself and I'm not going to do it in this bed."

Anne's fair skin colored, but her voice was firm when she replied. "Moses said I was to call him when you need assistance. He and Rufus are right outside." She turned on her heel and left the room.

Anne walked out onto the dogtrot, and saw Moses and Rufus approaching.

"Good morning, Mz. Anne. How be Massa Trace this mornin'?" Moses asked as he removed his battered straw hat.

Anne did not meet Moses eyes. "Good morning. I'm not sure but he needs some assistance."

The two men exchanged looks. Moses nodded. "Yes'um. I go right on in if that be awright wit you."

"Of course. I am going to cook some breakfast. We could all use a good meal." Anne turned back to the house.

"I done took keer of the hosses," Moses told Anne as she filled their plates with fried potatoes, eggs and bacon. Placing a biscuit on top, she handed the plates to them.

She filled another plate but put less food on it. "I'll take Trace's breakfast into him. He may need some help."

"Don' you furgit to eat, Mz. Anne. You's gonna need all your strength to keep Massa Trace down for a spell."

Two days later, Trace stood in the dog trot watching Rufus running from the fields toward the house, Dog at his heels. The animal had taken up permanent residence at the farm.

"Massa Trace, Massa, Trace! The sheriffs, they be comin' down the road. What you reckon they want?"

"I don't know Rufus, but there's nothing for you to worry about. We have all the necessary papers signed and witnessed. Go back and tell your grandpa everything is all right."

Rufus disappeared into the thicket as two riders approached the farm. As they drew near, the sunlight reflected off metal objects pinned to the men's shirts. *It's the sheriff all right.* He vaguely remembered the doctor had said something about reporting the attack to the law.

The men drew up to the hitch rail and Trace stepped down from the porch.

"Howdy. Light down and rest yourselves and your horses." Trace offered the invitation, because he knew the men would not dismount until he did.

"Much obliged," returned the taller of the two men. He came out of the saddle with practiced ease, indicating he had spent at lot of time on horseback. He stepped forward and offered his hand. "I take it you are Trace Burdette. I'm Sheriff Tom Dawson, and this is my deputy, Hiram Jones."

"Glad to make your acquaintance, Sheriff." Trace searched his memory for a family by the name of Dawson but could not recall them.

The men exchanged handshakes, all the while sizing each other up without being obvious about it. The sheriff looked to be nearing middle age, but his body was lean and muscled. His dark hair and thick mustache were sprinkled with gray. Jones was younger but he was running to fat. His belly hung over his belt and he had the makings of a double chin.

"Let's take some weight off our feet." Trace indicated the benches on the porch.

Anne appeared in the dog trot. "May I offer you some refreshment, gentlemen? I just made a fresh pot of coffee."

The men were on their feet. The sheriff and his deputy quickly removed their hats.

"Good day, Mz. Michaels." The sheriff caught his mistake and apologized. "I'm sorry; I forgot your name is Burdette now. It's good to see you ma'am. And a cup of coffee sounds mighty good."

"No need to apologize Sheriff. And do sit down. I'll be out with the coffee in a few minutes."

Dawson turned to Trace. "Doc tells me you were attacked by the Jackson boys and they stole your guns and your money. Doc said you might have some memory loss. If you remember what happened, I'd like to hear the whole story."

"My memory is still a little fuzzy, but I haven't forgotten I was jumped and who jumped me," Trace said, his voice hard. "That crutch of Job's 'bout broke my skull."

"Doc said you took some whacks on your shoulders and back, too."

Trace nodded. "Anne says I'm black and blue down to my waist."

Anne appeared with a tray loaded with a coffee pot and mugs. "I will fetch cream and sugar if you need it."

"No, ma'am," the officers said in unison.

Trace knew Anne tired easily, and he took the tray from her and placed it on a vacant chair.

"Thank you," Anne favored her husband with a smile.

"If you gentlemen will excuse me, I have bread dough to see to."

Waiting until Anne was inside the house, Dawson took up the story of the attack. "You want to file charges?"

"No. No sense in costing the county the expense of a trial. We both know what the outcome would be."

The lawman did not answer immediately but took a tobacco sack and cigarette papers from the breast pocket of his shirt. He offered it to Trace and the deputy who shook their heads. Dawson built a smoke, and touched a Lucifer to the end. With smoke streaming from his nostrils, he looked full at Trace.

"That's the trouble, Burdette, folks don't want to work with the law. How can we ever get Texas back on her feet if the citizens try to take the law into their own hands?"

Not waiting for an answer, he continued, "I don't know what you've heard about me, Burdette, but I don't cotton to lawbreakers whether they be Texans or Yankees."

"I don't really know anything about you, Sheriff, except I heard you used to be a Ranger. But I do know I wouldn't have a chance in court against the Jacksons. My major concern is my rifle. I want it back."

"Yes, I served with the Rangers awhile before I joined up with Terry. I heard about the weapon. And I don't blame you for feelin' the way you do. There's little argument the Jackson's took it, but I don't want you doin' anything foolish. I plan on riding over to the Jackson place and have a talk with them boys."

A surprised look passed over Trace's face, replaced by a slight grin, but there was no mirth in his voice when he answered. "That's sounds like a good idea to me. When do you want to go?"

"You're in no shape to ride. Doc said that head wound could cause you more than a mite of trouble. Me and Hiram can handle it. What about the money and your side arm?"

"Forget the money, sheriff. They've probably spent it by now. I would like to have my revolver back since it is army issue, but the rifle is more important to me."

Anne returned to the dog trot. "Dinner will be ready shortly. You are more than welcome to join us."

Trace seconded the invitation. "Yeah, there's plenty of food and Anne is a real fine cook."

The sheriff grinned. "I know Mz Anne fixes the best fried chicken I ever tasted. She always brings it to the church picnic. We appreciate the invite, but if we want to get to the Jackson place and back to Anderson before dark, we'd best be movin' on."

Anne watched from the window as the lawmen rode away. Her hand went to her abdomen where a slight bulge was beginning to show. She wondered if the sheriff had noticed and, if he had, would he spread it around that Anne Michaels Burdette was in the family way? She did not think so. The sheriff did not impress her as a man who engaged in gossip. After all, she was a *married* woman.

# CHAPTER SEVEN

WHILE TRACE RECUPERATED FROM HIS injuries, Moses and Rufus chopped weeds from the cotton. The tender young plants were not as tall as they should have been, but with adequate rainfall and hot summer nights, they would soon catch up.

Moses and Rufus were good workers and needed a minimum of instruction. The two men more than earned the meager wage Trace paid them. The thought of money forced Trace to think of his shrinking bank balance. With careful management, his funds should last until the cotton crop was sold.

His thoughts were interrupted when Anne appeared in the dog trot carrying the water bucket. Her condition was obvious now. Her slender figure was filling out, and the worried look was gone from her face. Her cheeks were flushed from the heat, and stray curls had escaped from the bun at the nape of her neck. *No wonder Alvin fell in love with her. She is a mighty pretty woman.* Trace would not allow himself to dwell on their platonic relationship. He would keep the bargain he had made with Anne. Maybe after the baby was born . . .

"Why don't you sit down and rest a spell. I'll get the water for you."

Anne smiled and handed him the bucket. "Thank you. I think I will sit down for a few minutes. The pies are not ready to come out of the oven."

Trace carried the bucket to the kitchen. He poured a cup of the cool water and carried it to Anne. When she smiled, the dimple in her left check came to life. Before his thoughts could go any farther, Trace stepped off the porch. Turning back to her, he suggested, "You've been working in that hot kitchen all morning. Why don't you fix something I can take to the men, and I'll eat with them. I want to make sure Moses doesn't get overheated. I don't know his age, but he has to be up there. And I need to talk to Rufus, too. They both know a lot about farming that I've forgotten."

The appreciation in Anne's eyes was plain to see. "If you're sure you don't want a hot meal . . ." Trace nodded and Anne continued. "There is plenty of ham, and the pies will be cool enough to cut by the time the yams finish baking."

"You should rest this afternoon."

"Perhaps I will lie down for a bit."

Trace followed Anne into the house and helped her remove the pies from the oven.

"They sure smell good," Trace sniffed the spicy aroma.

"I'll cut you a slice as soon as they cool," she offered.

Trace grinned. "That's a tempting offer, but I'll wait and eat with the men."

The hungry men devoured every morsel of the food that Anne prepared.

"Miz Anne am sho a fine cook," Moses said as he wiped his mouth with a rag he carried in his pocket.

"Sho is," Rufus added.

"Yes, she is. I'm lucky she agreed to marry me."

"Massa Trace,' Rufus spoke up, "the cotton be all finished. I see Mz Anne's kitchen garden be weedy. It be alright if'n I tend it for her?"

"Yes, I know she would appreciate it. She's not used to that kind of work besides . . . ." Pregnancy was a subject that was not discussed among men folk.

A loud pounding woke Trace from a sound sleep.

"Massa Trace, Massa Trace, come quick. Some mens are ridin' through the cotton field."

It was as black as pitch in the loft. Grabbing his pants from the chair, Trace fumbled for his boots. By the time they reached the dog trot, he could hear the sounds of the men and horses. Their voices were muffled, and Trace figured they were wearing masks. He started toward the field on the run.

"Massa Trace yo be keerful. Them mens got guns and they shoot yo dead."

Trace swore under his breath. The sheriff had not returned his rifle or side arm. Without weapons, he was powerless to stop the devastation. The old musket he found hidden in the loft would not be an effective weapon against repeater rifles. The wooden stock was scarred and the barrel pitted from years of neglect. He wished he had taken time to clean and test it. By the time he reached the field, he could make out the shadows of the mounted riders. There appeared to be five of them. A sliver of moonlight shone briefly on a rider on a buckskin horse. He was wearing a black hood over his head.

Trace motioned to Moses and Rufus to stay hidden. Their eyes were wide with fright.

"We're 'bout finished here," the rider on the buckskin called out.

"Let's git the kitchen garden," another answered. "That'll fix 'em good."

*I can't let them do that. It will break Anne's heart. She sets such store by it.* Trace stepped into the open. "You bastards! Too cowardly to show your faces."

Rufus was beside him and pulled him to safety as a shot rang out. With a loud rebel yell, the riders spurred their horses and disappeared in the brush bordering the road.

Trace trembled with anger and frustration. He had gone through the war, which produced more horror than any human should have to witness. He returned to Texas, which he did not want to do, after Alvin was killed. He met Anne and circumstances changed. He found himself wanting to remain on the land that had been in the Burdette family for three generations. A new life would soon come into the world to continue the line. The beating by the Jackson brothers served to strengthen his decision to remain.

Now, with his crop destroyed and his finances running low, how would he take care of a wife and baby? Perhaps he could secure a loan from the bank. The faces of his father and mother appeared in his mind's eye. Although there were plenty of hard times, Burdette land had never been mortgaged. There had to be another way.

"Trace! Trace! What is happening?" Anne was standing in the dog trot wearing a robe, her hair hanging down her back in a long braid.

Mindful of her condition and ignoring the ruined crop, Trace hurried to her side. "It's all right, Anne." Gathering her in his arms, he awkwardly patted her back. "Everything is going to be all right." How could he tell her she had married a man whose enemies hated him so much that they were trying to destroy him?

\*    \*    \*

"If you feel like going to town tomorrow, we could spend the night there and come home the next day," Trace said as he dried the supper dishes. He had finally convinced Anne to accept his help with some of the household chores. She had not complained, but he knew she was not strong and tired easily. Surely, he would soon find a woman to help her.

Anne's face broke into a smile. "Oh, yes! I would love to see Poppa, and we do need a few things."

"Good. We'll leave right after breakfast. Moses and Rufus can take care of the evening chores."

Anne retired to her bedroom to prepare for the trip. The clothing she had altered would soon need to be replaced with new garments. How could she ask Trace to purchase what she needed? Her father would be glad to provide for her, but it was no longer his place to do so.

Her problem was solved the next morning before they left the farm. After placing her portmanteau in the back of the wagon, Trace turned to help her. "I know there are . . . there are womanly things you need. You can get them at Stone's Mercantile. Tell the clerk to add your purchases to the bill. And don't be afraid to get everything you need."

Anne's face showed a faint hint of color, but her voice was steady when she answered. "Thank you, Trace. I appreciate your generosity."

A frown flitted across Trace's countenance. "Anne, you are my wife. It is my duty to provide for you." The frown disappeared to be replaced by a smile. "Besides, a pretty woman should have pretty things."

When Anne was settled at the hotel, Trace walked to the sheriff's office. He found Tom Dawson seated behind his desk sorting through a stack of wanted posters.

"Burdette." Dawson rose and offered his hand.

"Howdy, Sheriff." The men shook hands, each giving the gesture meaning. "You found my weapons yet?" Trace's voice carried a hard edge.

Dawson continued standing behind his desk. After a minute, he answered. "Not yet. I talked to the Jackson brothers and they denied having anything to do with your *accident*. I believe your story but without witnesses, it's your word against theirs." He held up his hand. "Now, before you get all riled up, I want you to know I'm still investigating. We may be able to get them weapons back after all."

"That's about what I expected." Trace did not try to conceal the bitterness in his voice. "But I have some news for you."

"Pull up a chair and tell me about it." Dawson sat down behind the desk.

Trace straddled the wooden chair and faced Dawson. "Two nights ago, five masked riders destroyed my cotton crop. Rode their horses through it and yelled like a bunch of Comanches while they were doing it."

Dawson's face went white. "My God! It's started. I been afraid of this. Did you recognize any of them?"

"I couldn't swear to their identity, but one of them rode a buckskin horse. I might recognize his voice if I heard it again. He seemed to be the leader."

"There ain't many buckskin horses in these parts. Should be easy to find them."

Trace's laughter held no mirth. "Fellow can always do a little horse tradin' when it's called for. I plan to buy a shotgun today, sheriff. It won't replace my rifle, but I can burn a few tail feathers if they come around again."

"Trace, I'm mighty sorry about your troubles. I'll do all I can to help you." He pulled a ruled tablet from the desk drawer. "I'm going to make out a report, and I need all the information you can give me."

Trace returned to the hotel and found Anne in the lobby engaged in conversation with a young woman. *Must be the schoolteacher John told us about.*

Anne looked up and smiled. "Oh, there is my husband now. Trace, I would like you to meet Miss Regina Mills. She's the school teacher Poppa told us about. Miss Mills is from Indiana. She taught in a Christian school there."

Trace doffed his hat and made a slight bow. "Please to meet you, ma'am."

"How do you do, Mr. Burdette."

She offered her hand and Trace felt the smooth soft skin. *Not the hands of a woman who has ever done hard work.*

"Mrs. Burdette has been telling me you live on a farm."

"Yes, ma'am. 'bout ten miles out of town."

"Before I came to Anderson, I spent several weeks with my aunt and uncle who live on a farm near Marshall. The countryside is lovely here."

"It is real pretty in the spring, what with all the flowers bloomin'." Trace was never comfortable with small talk, especially when women were involved.

Anne gestured toward the chairs. "I'm sure we would be more comfortable if we sat down." Her feet swelled if she stood for any length of time.

"Yes, of course," Regina replied.

Regina smoothed her skirts while Anne shifted in her chair until she found a satisfactory position. When they were settled, Trace spoke. "If you ladies will excuse me, I want to speak with John." Turning to Regina, he added, "It was a pleasure to meet you, ma'am. I hope your stay in Anderson is a pleasant one."

"Thank you. It was nice meeting you, too. I'm looking forward to my teaching duties."

Trace nodded and strode toward the desk where John had his head buried in a ledger. He looked up and grinned. "Looks like Annie and the new teacher have hit it off."

"Yeah, I sure hope so. Anne needs women friends and the women here in town . . . ,"

"That's been a worry to me too." John snapped the ledger closed.

Trace lowered his voice and asked, "Can we go in the back? I need to talk to you in private."

"Sure thing. I'll make us some coffee."

While the coffee was boiling, Trace filled John in on the destruction of his cotton field. "Of course Anne knows but I don't want to upset her by talking about finding out who was behind it. The sheriff plans to look into it, or so he says."

"He's a good man, Trace. He will try to help you, but it appears to me he don't get much cooperation from people—town folk or farmers."

"That's what I figure. I plan to do some scoutin' around for that buckskin horse. Course, whoever rode it knows I saw him, so he might have got rid of it, but it's the only lead I have."

John hesitated a moment before speaking. "I know it's none of my business, but the loss of your crop is bound to hurt you financially. If there is any way I can help out, I'd be glad to."

"I appreciate your offer, John. I'm not sure how it's all going to work out, but I intend to take care of Anne and the baby just like I promised." His features set and grim, Trace's blue eyes took on a wintry hue.

Anne and Regina were deep in discussion of the benefits of living in a large city. Since Anne had been to San Antonio before the war, her memories were those of a child. She was anxious to hear about the theaters, the shops, the great churches, all the attractions she had read about.

"Yes," Regina answered, "Indianapolis has many places of interest. The city is coming out of the . . . the depression brought on by the war." She shifted in her seat. While she was with her relatives in Marshall, she had ample opportunity to witness the bitterness and hatred the South felt for the North.

Anne placed her hand on Regina's arm. "I understand. As you will find out, if you haven't already, Trace fought for the Union. He stayed in the army and didn't intend to come back to Texas, but his brother died and left him the farm."

Trace joined the women but gave no indication that he had heard Anne's remark. "Do you feel up to doing your shopping or would you rather wait until morning?"

"Oh, I'm fine. If I do the shopping now, it will give us an earlier start back to the farm." She turned to Regina. "I'm going to shop for the baby. Would you like to join me?" Her face colored and she added, "If you don't think it would be inappropriate?" After all, the teacher was an unmarried woman.

"Oh, I would be delighted. I am anxious to see what is available since I will no doubt need things from time to time."

"I will escort you to the mercantile and take care of the supplies," Trace offered.

The two women browsing among the yard goods turned around. Their smiles disappeared; replaced by frowns. Two pairs of eyes focused on Anne's expanding waistline.

It was bound to happen sooner or later. Anne lifted her chin and spoke in a pleasant voice. "Hello, ladies. Regina, have you met Mrs. Crow and Mrs. Parks? Miss Mills has come to Anderson to teach at the Negro school."

"We seen her in church. How do, Miss Mills." Mrs. Crow, a tall thin woman with a tight knot of graying dark hair, acknowledged.

*What an appropriate name.* Immediately, Regina chastised herself for such uncharitable thoughts.

Mrs. Parks was her friend's opposite. Short and plump, her blonde hair had escaped its pins and loose curls framed her face. "How do, Miss Mills."

"It's nice to see you, ladies." Regina smiled.

"We'd best be goin' Gladys. Good day." Mrs. Crow grabbed her companion's arm and hurried her out of the store.

Anne selected materials for the baby's layette plus material for two skirts and waists plus undergarments. Regina was surprised to see the variety of colors and patterns in the bolts of calico. She wore calico when she helped Nancy in the kitchen on the maid's day off or when working in the flower garden. From spending time with her relatives on their farm outside Marshall, she knew that calico was the backbone of a frontier woman's wardrobe.

"Poppa, can you come to Sunday dinner?" Anne worried that her father was not eating properly.

"I'd like that Annie. Besides, you ever know me to turn down one of your home cooked meals?"

Anne smiled. "No." Turning to Regina, she asked, "Would you care to join us? I'm sure Poppa would be glad of company on the way to the farm and back to the hotel."

"Oh, that would be lovely, but are you sure it won't be too much trouble?"

"Of course not. As you know, I enjoy cooking. Besides, it will give us a chance to visit."

\*     \*     \*

Their wagon laden with supplies, Trace and Anne left Anderson early the next morning. Late spring temperatures climbed quickly.

"I spoke with your father about you staying with him when I'm away." Trace kept his gaze focused on the horses.

Anne was quick to point out her father's viewpoint.

"Poppa told me you did and urged me to come and stay at the hotel. Naturally, he is concerned about me. And he understands our situation."

Trace caught Anne's reference to *our* situation. Anne might be young, but she had a good head on her shoulders. He was lucky to have a wife who gave him her total support. "I need to make a trip to Brenham next week. I may be gone a few days. When John comes for dinner on Sunday, why don't you plan on going back with him?"

"If you think that is best. I don't mind saying that I look forward to visiting with Regina. Oh, not that I am lonely on the farm, it's just that . . ."

Trace freed a hand from the reins and placed it on top of hers, which were clasped in her lap. "I understand. It will give you a chance to rest, too. Moses and Rufus can look after things."

"I will do some baking and fix a few things for them before I leave. There is a large piece of ham which should last them for several days." Anne took her responsibility for their welfare to heart. *After all, they are like part of the family.*

Anne and Trace were in the kitchen when they heard the sound of hoof beats; horses that seemed to keep cadence as they approached the farmhouse.

*Must be five or six of them.* Trace stood in the dog trot watching as the riders came into view. The bright sunshine intensified the blue color of their uniforms. Cavalry! Wonder what they're doing in this area? He counted four troopers, two abreast with an officer in the lead.

Trace heard a slight shuffling of footsteps. From the corner of his eye, he saw Moses and Rufus vanish behind the house. He had just given them their instructions for the day. Although their papers were in order, their friendship with Trace did not extend to the U. S. Cavalry. Too many cases of violence had been turned over to the military courts where they either stalled in the system or were dismissed.

The officer called a halt. His gold bars glinted in the sunlight. *Must be important they sent a captain to handle it.* Trace stepped off the porch. "Howdy. Light and rest your saddles."

The captain handed his reins to the sergeant who rode up beside him. Dismounting, he removed his gauntlets and offered his hand. "I'm Captain Phillip Morgan, Fifth Military District, Galveston. Is this the Burdette farm? We are looking for Trace Burdette."

"I'm Trace Burdette. What can I do for you, Captain?"

Morgan's grip was strong. Traced judged him to be in his forties. Leathery skin and keen gray eyes told him the captain had seen many years of hard service.

"The Army has some business to discuss with you, *Sergeant* Burdette." A grin played across the captain's stern features.

Trace's expression grew puzzled at the reference to his former rank. He was honorably discharged and there had been no contact with the army since he left Fort Riley.

"It is a highly confidential matter. Is there a place we can talk in private?"

"Yes sir." Old habits die hard. "We can talk in the parlor."

The captain nodded. "Dismiss the men, Sergeant."

"Yes sir." The man saluted and began issuing orders.

Anne was in the kitchen mixing bread dough. She had tied an old sheet around her waist and was up to her elbows in flour. When she looked up and saw Trace and Captain Morgan, her face flushed a bright red. "I . . . I didn't know we had a guest,"

"It's all right, Anne. This is Captain Morgan from the Fifth Military District in Galveston. Captain, my wife."

Anne tried to tidy her appearance as the captain removed his hat. "Don't be upset, Mrs. Burdette. I apologize for barging in on you like this. I came to discuss some business with Sergeant . . . that is, Mr. Burdette."

"We will be in the parlor, Anne."

"I'll come right to the point, Burdette. You are aware of the turmoil and violence that's going on all over this part of Texas."

Trace nodded but did not speak.

"The Army is here to help keep law and order. We are often responsible for trying deadlocked civil suits by military tribunal. This takes an inordinate amount of time and the end results are often unsatisfactory. The answer is to curtail the events in the first place. Of course, we get little cooperation from the citizens." Morgan paused to relight his cheroot.

The destruction of Trace's cotton crop was more than ample proof that the captain was right. He was certain the sheriff had not reported the incident to the courts. Why was the Army seeking him out?

Anne appeared in the parlor door carrying a tray set with two cups of coffee, cream and sugar. She had removed the sheet from around her waist and tied her appearance. "Gentlemen, I made fresh coffee and there are some cookies, too."

Trace rose quickly and took the tray from her. Captain Morgan rose from his seat. "I didn't mean to interrupt your duties, ma'am. But it is mighty hospitable of you, and I appreciate it. It's been a long ride from the fort."

"You are quite welcome, Captain. Now, if you will excuse me, I need to see to my bread making."

Morgan helped himself to coffee and placed two cookies on his saucer. "Your wife is a lovely woman. Is she a local person?"

"Yes, her father owns a hotel in Anderson. But I believe they lived in San Antonio before the war." That was all the information Trace was going to provide about his wife.

There was a lull in the conversation while the men enjoyed the refreshments. Morgan placed his cup and saucer on the tray. He pursed his lips for a moment; then spoke. "This is what the army has in mind. Your service during the war was exemplary, and we understand you intended to make a career of the army. Then your brother was killed and you came back to Texas. You married and decided to remain on the farm. You do not intend to go back into the military. Is that correct?"

Trace' eyes narrowed. Where was this all leading? "Yes, Captain, my soldierin' days are over. Just what is it the army wants from me?"

"We need your services, Burdette." He held up his hand.

"Wait! Hear me out before you turn us down. We don't expect you to reenlist. No, this is a special assignment. You will still be a civilian, but under the supervision of the U.S. Army. The details have not been completely worked out, depending on your acceptance. You can remain here in Grimes County, most of the time anyway. Your status will be equivalent to that of sergeant and you will receive the same pay."

The captain paused and Trace took the opportunity to break in. "What is it the army wants me to do?" He had an uneasy feeling about the duties he would be asked to perform.

"We are asking you to work undercover to help us learn who is behind the violence and vigilante movements in this part of the state."

Trace stared at the captain. "In other words, you are asking me to be a spy."

Morgan's face flushed but he looked Trace in the eye when he answered. "Yes. We know that you are not on the best of terms with some of your neighbors. We know that your crops were destroyed by vigilantes. We also know your sheriff is honest but gets little cooperation from the people. We know that you are watched from time to time, especially when you move about."

"As I mentioned, the details need to be finalized if you accept the assignment. And, we hope you will. We need your help."

\*   \*   \*

Trace placed his knife and fork in his empty plate. He dabbed at his lips with the hem-stitched napkin that Anne insisted they use. "That was a mighty fine meal, Anne."

Anne smiled. Trace was always thoughtful. "Thank you."

"I enjoy cooking, especially since you are so easy to please."

Trace paused. It was time to discuss the army's offer. "Anne, we need to talk about the captain's visit today."

"Whatever you chose to tell me is fine with me."

"I didn't talk with you about it after he left, because I wanted to run it through my mind first. It boils down to this. The army wants me to work for them as a special agent." He paused to watch the puzzled expression on Anne's face.

"Special agent? What does that mean?"

"I would be a civilian employed by the army and receive my former sergeant's pay. My savings are getting low, and since the *vigilantes* destroyed our crop, I need to find a way to make some money. It would mean that I have to be away from home, sometimes overnight. I wouldn't leave you alone with just Moses and Rufus. I will find somebody to stay with you."

Anne chewed her lip for a moment. "I can always go to the hotel and stay with Poppa."

"Yeah, I thought about that, but as your *time* comes, you can't travel to town very often, if at all."

"Maybe it would be better if I were in town close to the doctor." At Trace's concerned look, she hastened to add, "Don't worry, everything is fine. But as you said, later it will be harder for me to go to town."

Nodding his head in agreement, Trace answered, "That makes sense but for the present you will need help."

"Can you tell me anymore about this special agent thing?"

"Not a lot. Some of it is classified information, but I may need to go to Brenham to make my reports. The army is going to send another agent to work with me, but I don't know when he will be here."

"I think you've made up your mind, Trace. I want you to know that I will not interfere in your work. My part is to give you all the support I can."

If Anne's eyes were a little misty, Trace pretended not to notice. He rose from the table and went to her side. He helped her from her chair and gently embraced her. Smoothing her hair, he bent and kissed her cheek.

"You are a wonderful woman, Anne. I'm sorry Alvin didn't live so that you could share your life with him."

"I've made my peace with Alvin's death. It was not meant to be, and you have given me a reason to go on. I know you will love the baby and care for it as if it were your own. Maybe some day . . . ."

No further words were spoken. Both knew that Anne was referring to a child of their union. Trace smiled inwardly at the thought. Yes, he and Anne could have a real marriage. He was very fond of her although he was not in love with her. His mother had told him he must respect and like a woman first and love would come.

*　　*　　*

"The meal was delicious," Regina complimented her hostess.

"Thank you," Anne replied. "My mother was an excellent teacher. I enjoy cooking and I have a very good helper." She smiled as Trace tried to look unconcerned. Most men considered household tasks strictly women's work.

John nodded. "Yes, my Maurine had a magic touch and she passed it on to our daughter."

Regina and John had arrived shortly before noon. Anne had insisted on using the things from her hope chest and, under her supervision, Trace had set the table. He had also fetched water and done the heavy lifting of kettles and pots.

"Let me help you clear," Regina offered.

"You are our guest," Anne resisted.

"That doesn't mean I can't help you. I'm sure the men would like to have their tobacco in the parlor."

"Yeah, lassie, that would be nice." John agreed. He often reverted back to his Scottish brogue.

When they were settled in the parlor, John brought up the incident that had occurred in Prairie Lea several weeks ago. A story had gone around that two soldiers shot two citizens and ordered another man to leave the county.

"I don't believe the soldiers shot those men unless they had a good reason. That's not the army way, especially in peacetime. Although I guess you could hardly call this peacetime." A touch of bitterness filtered through Trace's voice.

"The way I hear it," John continued, "Governor Throckmorton appealed to General Griffin to investigate the shooting, and the general told him the army was innocent. Said for Throckmorton to enforce the law or stand aside and let the army do it."

"The general does have a point considering all the trouble in these parts. That Navasota situation where the two men were accused of killing the soldiers, and the army sent a detachment to arrest them, caused a near riot. The officer in charge, I believe his name is Sutherland, used his head and defused it although he jeopardized his mission. I heard later that some citizen wrote the governor and apologized. Claimed the whole thing was caused by drunks and rowdies."

"That worries me some, Trace. This job you're taking with the army could be very dangerous."

The expression on Trace's face hardened. "I won't deny that but I need the money, and I don't see any other way to earn it."

As the women worked, Regina brought up her teaching assignment. "I've spoken with Mr. Shields. He is the Freedmen's Bureau representative in Anderson. The Thompson family has donated an old cabin at edge of town to use as a school. It is being renovated and I should be able to begin teaching in a couple of weeks."

"Oh, that is wonderful news. I know you're anxious to get started." Anne slid the stack of plates into the dishwater.

"Yes, I am. I have been studying the text books and making outlines. I'm so grateful the books arrived in plenty of time for me to review them before school begins." Regina's voice reflected her enthusiasm.

"Have you found permanent accommodations?"

"Not yet. I enjoy staying at your father's establishment but meals are somewhat of a problem. I have eaten at most of the restaurants in town and some of them serve decent food. But, I don't like leaving the hotel for breakfast. I'm not sure I want to rent a place of my own, but boarding with a private family . . . ," her voice trailed off.

Anne nodded. "I understand. Living alone could be . . . well, a little . . . difficult. Some of the other hotels have dining rooms. What about the Fanthrop Inn? Poppa would understand if you wanted to move."

"It's too far from the schoolhouse. Besides, I don't think Mrs. Fanthrop is too fond of the idea of a single woman staying there on a permanent basis. Mr. Shields said he would check around for me."

When the dishes were finished and everything put back in its proper place, the women joined the men in the parlor. From the look on their faces, Anne suspected they had not been engaged in idle conversation.

John's expression grew thoughtful. "Trace, since you want to go to Brenham in a day or two, Anne could ride to the hotel with us this afternoon. It would save you a trip to town. That is, if Annie is agreeable."

"Would that the alright with you, Anne?"

"I . . . I don't know. There isn't a lot of food left over, and I need to provide for Moses and Rufus plus your trail supplies."

"Don't worry about that. Before you came, they survived on my cooking. I can put a few things together for them and myself."

"There are some biscuits and a couple of loaves of bread in the larder."

"It's all settled then. I'll come through town just as soon as I take care of the business in Brenham. You've been working pretty hard. Try to rest while I'm gone," Trace urged.

Anne smiled at her husband. She was lucky he was considerate of her condition. She had heard a lot of husbands were not.

"Mr. Burdette," Regina spoke up. "I am delighted to have the opportunity to visit with Anne, and I promise I will see that she takes very good care of herself."

"I appreciate that, ma'am. And I know John will keep an eye on the two of you."

"If you will excuse me, I need to pack a few things." Anne left the room.

"Let me help you," Regina offered and hurried after Anne.

As he watched the women, John turned to Trace. "I'm so glad that Anne and Miss Mills are becoming good friends. I don't know what she's heard of your situation, but it hasn't seemed to make any difference."

Trace nodded. "I have a feeling Regina Mills is not easily influenced by what other people say. I think she's a woman who makes up her own mind and chooses her own friends."

"I think you're right," John agreed.

John and Regina walked to the buggy leaving Anne and Trace alone in the dog trot. Anne broke the awkward silence. "Trace, I know the trip could be dangerous. Please be careful."

Trace grinned and gathered her in a clumsy embrace. "Don't you worry about me. I'll be fine. You take care of yourself and the baby." He picked up her portmanteau and they joined John and Regina. Before handing her up into buggy, he kissed her on the check.

*     *     *

Trace rose at dawn in order to get an early start to Brenham. He found the men in the barn feeding the horses. "Mornin' Massa Trace," they chorused.

Trace had tried to discourage Moses and Rufus from calling him "Massa," but the habit was deeply ingrained.

"Morning," he returned their greeting. He was carrying the milk pail and set it down outside the cow's stall.

"You want I should milk her?" Rufus asked.

"Not this morning, Rufus. I have some thinking to do, and I seem to do it better if my hands are busy. You can gather the eggs if there are any."

Trace entered the stall where the cow was munching contentedly on a small mound of hay. "Good morning, Flossie," he greeted the animal with a pat on her broad rump. She swished her tail and gave a soft bawl. As the milk foamed into the pail, Trace focused on the trip to Brenham. He would need to keep his guard up, because there were numerous bands of misfits roaming the countryside. A lone rider would be tempting prey for the unscrupulous ones. He finished the milking and set the bucket on the stool. Motioning for Moses and Rufus to come near, he told them he would be leaving for Brenham right after breakfast.

Moses and Rufus exchanged glances, their expressions telling Trace they were uneasy with the news. "Anne is going to stay with her father at the hotel while I'm gone. Shouldn't be more than two or three days. There won't be much for you to do except take care of the animals and keep an eye on the place. Keep your eyes open and if any hostile riders show up find yourselves a good hiding place. I don't want either of you to get hurt."

"But Massa Trace, what if'n them mens try to steal everthin?"

"Just stay hid and let them take what ever they want." Trace cautioned. "Remember, they might not stop at just disabling you. I don't have to tell you they might do worse."

# CHAPTER EIGHT

S TARING AT HER REFLECTION IN the mirror, Regina contemplated the gown she had chosen for her first day of school. The burgundy bengaline with its white collar and pearl buttons was the least fashionable in her wardrobe. She had eliminated one of the three petticoats in the interest of comfort. Her sturdy black boots would protect her from the rough terrain on the walk to the school house. She needed to find housing closer as soon as possible. Mr. Shields had made inquiries at a local boarding house but found only male occupants and quickly crossed it off the list.

Mary Fanthrop Stone, the daughter of the owners of the Fantrop Inn, had spoken to her after church last Sunday. She apologized for her mother's reluctance to rent accommodations to Regina. Regina graciously accepted her apology and explained that the inn really was too far from the school. Mrs. Stone had volunteered to help Regina find housing but so far nothing had come of it.

Putting her problems aside, Regina picked up her portmanteau filled with school supplies. She straightened her skirts, took a deep breath and closed the door behind her. The small room smelled peculiar and dust mites drifted in the stale air. The building had once been a store house and Regina identified the odor of rancid meat. She hurried to the windows which had been installed when the building was repaired. There was no glass or covering over the open spaces which had been fitted with tight wooden shutters. Bright sunshine flooded the room as the wind began to stir the offensive odor.

The room was divided by a center aisle. Regina stopped to survey the crude desks and chairs. She could not call them desks. They were simply tables which could be shared by two students. Rough hewn benches provided the seating. At the front of the room sat a large wood desk that must have come from a business office. Her eyes wide with shock, Regina saw there was no blackboard. How on earth could she teach the children without a way to write down the lessons? To make matters worse, there were no slates in the supplies she had been given. The problem had to be solved as soon as possible. She would call on Mr. Shields right after school.

"Good morning," Regina walked around the desk and smiled at the small group of boys and girls. The children, their black faces scrubbed and shining, were dressed in ragged and patched clothing that had been starched and ironed. She counted six girls who wore their hair in pigtails. The three boys' kinky hair was cropped close to their heads. Regina guessed their ages from six to ten years.

"I am very happy to see all of you. My name is Miss Mills, and I will be your teacher. You need to tell me your names so that we may get acquainted. Please move to the front of the room and sit in the first rows of seats. I will start with the first row on this side." Regina pointed to the right side of the room. "The seat you chose will be the seat you will sit in for the school term. When you give me your name, I will enter it in this book." Regina held up the ledger in which she would record all the information about the students.

Regina, stunned to learn several of the students had no last name. Two of the boys were named Cox, Joseph and Adam. Their mother, Alice, was one of Regina's night students. The other boy was called Willie, no last name. The six girls were Bessie and Lucy Jones, Mable Evans, Cassie, no last name. Emma, no last name, and Pearl Butler. Most of the children were not sure of their ages and Regina decided she would try to contact the parents. Perhaps they were not aware they could choose a last name. Some of them used the name of their former owners, others picked names that appealed to them.

The better part of Regina's day was taken up with details. She explained what the students were going to study. When she illustrated the textbooks and supplies they would use, it was not difficult to determine that most of the children had never been exposed to books, paper or pencils.

"Miss Mills," John Michaels greeted her as she entered the hotel lobby. "How did it go today?" He took in the slump of her shoulders and tired expression in her eyes. The young lady from the north had learned more today than her students.

"Good afternoon, Mr. Michaels. I guess it went well enough, but it is much different than . . . ," Her voice tapered off and a slight blush colored her skin.

"I'm sure it is, but it will get better."

"Oh, yes sir. I know it will. The children are so eager to learn."

Regina slowly climbed the stairs to her room. The first day of school was always strenuous, but today had been the most difficult of her career. Her pupils in Indiana came from middle class families and had been taught proper deportment. Often first graders had vague ideas about learning to read and write. An exceptional few knew their letters. The grade levels were clearly defined and the curriculum outlined and enforced. Regina realized she had not given as much thought to teaching as she had of being independent. Leaving her home to go to the frontier to teach had seemed patriotic and exciting.

Her Yankee determination came to the rescue. I will not fail! I will not go back home!

A soft knock interrupted Regina's inner conflict. She sighed. It was probably Anne who was anxious to hear about her first day of school. Anne had told her that she had thought of becoming a teacher, but she knew her father needed her to help him with the hotel.

Regina opened the door to see Anne, an eager expression on her face. The woman's pregnancy was obvious, and she looked thin and frail.

"Come in and sit down," Regina invited. "That climb up the stairs must wear you out."

"Well, it is getting more difficult." Anne settled in the rocker while Regina sat on the edge of the bed and unbuttoned her boots. "You looked tired, Regina. Was it so very hard?"

Regina bit her lip. She was not going to lie to Anne, but neither did she want to sugar coat the heavy responsibility she had under taken. "Well, it was . . . very different from what I am used to. Everything at the school in Indiana is . . . is spelled out in great detail. The teacher knows exactly what is expected of her, and she is supposed to accomplish the goals the school has set."

Anne pursed her lips for a moment. "Perhaps the Reverend Foster could help you in some way. He graduated from a seminary and was formally ordained. And he is very understanding."

"That's an excellent idea, Anne. But before I can discuss the situation with him, I need to spend more time with the students."

\*    \*    \*

Thankful for an uneventful trip to Brenham, Trace rode into the small army post late the next afternoon. Surveying his surroundings, he saw that it was not typical of most army installations. There was no formal parade ground, and the buildings looked to be a collection of old business establishments. Evidently the army did not intend to establish a permanent post in Brenham. Several Negro troopers lounged in front of the converted barracks.

The sign over a small shop-like building read *Headquarters United States Army, Seventeenth Infantry Division.* Contrary to the usual frontier officer, the first lieutenant standing beside the desk was the epitome of the West Point graduate. His blue uniform was pressed, the trousers creased, and brass buttons shined. "What can I do for you, sir?" he asked as Trace approached.

"My name is Trace Burdette. Captain Morgan recruited me to work with the army as a civilian *scout.* Have you received any orders detailing my assignment?"

"Lieutenant Weatherford." He held out his hand. His grip was firm. "Yes, the captain spent the night here before going on to locate you. He filled me in and we discussed a set of S O P although you won't find them in the book."

Trace ginned. "No, I don't suppose you will."

"You're partner should arrive any day now," the lieutenant continued. "I understand that he wants to work undercover so I assume he will contact you."

"Can you tell me anything about him? His name, what he looks like, his background . . . ?"

"His name is Grady Hawkins although he is known to use an alias some of the time. He served in the Union army during the war and has been with the army in a civilian capacity since then. He's thirty years old, unmarried and very good with firearms."

"Sounds like a man I need on my side. Probably can teach me a trick or two." Trace was not adverse to learning new ways to stay alive.

After a short discussion concerning how and when he should send reports to the post which would be relayed to Galveston, when and how he would be paid, and other details, Trace prepared to take his leave of Lieutenant Weatherford.

"Before you leave town, Burdette, I think you should know that there are two cases of yellow fever in Brenham. It seems to have been brought here by travelers from Galveston. We have two doctors in Brenham and they are both trying to keep it from spreading and starting a panic. You need to warn the doctors in your area."

"Yellow fever! Good Lord! I haven't actually experienced it myself, but I know it is deadly. I'll contact the doctors in Navasota and Anderson just as soon as I get back." Trace thought of Anne and her advancing pregnancy. God forbid she should catch the deadly disease!

The aroma of supper cooking tickled Trace's nose. He had eaten a meal in the saddle in order to reach Brenham before dark. The town offered two or three small restaurants that he would check out later. It was too late to start back home. A lone rider was in enough danger in the daylight to say nothing of the dark. Besides, his horse was tired and needed tending. There was usually an empty cot or two at the livery where a weary rider could bunk for two bits or so.

As he rode toward the livery stable, Trace could see remnants of the fire that had nearly destroyed the town the year before. A local newspaper editor, D. L. McGrady, a Confederate who opposed the occupation, continuously wrote scathing editorials denouncing the federal authorities. McGrady was finally jailed. This culminated in a stand off between the townspeople and the black troopers. Later the same night, the troopers returned, looted the store and set it afire, and it spread to other buildings. Some army camps took advantage of the situation. Trace had seen the signs which proclaimed: "If this camp is molested, every house in the community will be burned."

How long will this go on? Maybe if these people had seen the carnage of the East and South, the broken bodies, the piles of amputated limbs, the faces of the soldiers, their clothing in tatters and the worst part of all, their faces. Thin, young faces that were lined and weary with fatigue, the look in their eyes that said they had seen sights that no human should have to see, and experienced events that no human should have to endure. Maybe, just maybe there would be less bitterness, less hostility and violence. As for Trace, he had seen enough to last him two lifetimes.

The livery stable was a run down barn and corral near the end of the main thoroughfare. Hard times lay heavy on the land and Trace again thanked the Lord for the opportunity for gainful employment. He had no delusions that the work would be dangerous but he had to take the risk. Tired from a hard day's ride, he slid from the saddle and entered the dark interior of the barn. The building smelled of years of accumulated dung, wet straw and the pungent odor of animal urine. A man walked toward him, dragging a stiff leg as he came.

"Howdy, stranger. Need your hoss took care of," he asked in a tired voice.

"Howdy. Yep, just be here for the night. Don't suppose you have an extra bunk you could spare?" Trace was thinking maybe it would be better to camp outside town rather than spend the night in the malodorous stable. Scenes of the places he had slept during the war flashed though his mind. *At least the place is better than a bloody battlefield.*

"Sure do. Cost you four bits. "Course I cain't grain 'im for that." The man spit a stream of tobacco juice on the hard packed floor.

"That'll do." Trace reached into his pocket and pulled out two coins.

"Name's Ollie," the man said as he took the money in his left hand and held out his right. Dirt and thick calluses covered the man's palms and his grip was strong.

"Trace Burdette. Know where a fella can find a decent meal that won't cost him a week's wages?"

The man grinned, showing tobacco stained teeth. "Reckon the Wagon Wheel be the best fur the money. Next to the general store on Main Street."

Two biscuits slathered in butter and two cups of strong coffee served Trace for breakfast. Not only did he want to conserve his dwindling resources, but he was eager to be on his way home. He knew Anne was with her father and Miss Mills was a good friend, but the pregnancy had not been easy. The next few months might prove even more difficult.

The air was still and an early morning mist hung over the landscape. No travelers were about and Trace let his thoughts wander. What did the future hold for him and Anne? With any luck, the army job would see them through until he could get back to farming. He had promised Anne's father that he would take care of her and raise the baby as his own. He hoped it would be a boy although he had never mentioned it to Anne.

"Hold up there!" A deep voice broke the silence as a rider rode out of the brush into the middle of the road.

Trace stiffened in the saddle, his eyes narrowing as he watched the stranger. The man sat tall in the saddle but his face was shadowed by the brim of his black Stetson. Trace brought his horse to a halt "Howdy."

"Might you be Trace Burdette?" the stranger asked.

The black gelding he rode and the dark clothing he wore gave Trace a sinister feeling. "Who's asking," he replied, his voice flat.

The rider pushed back his hat and a grin softened his features. "Don't spook, pard." He urged his mount closer. "I'm Grady Hawkins. Seems me and you are to partner up and help the army out." He extended his hand.

"I'm Trace Burdette. I been wonderin' when we would meet up."

"Why don't we get off the trail here and find us a place where we can palaver?" Grady turned his mount into the brush growing beside the road.

Trace studied Hawkins' back as they rode single file into the wooded area. He was broad shouldered and Trace judged him to be quite tall from the looks of his long legs. There was no question the man had spent most of his time in the saddle. He let the horse pick its way through the tangled underbrush, the reins held loosely in his hand.

The riders came upon a small clearing in the dense woods. The remnants of an old camp site were visible.

"Don't look like it's been used for a spell," Trace said.

"Looks that way. How 'bout we make a pot of coffee?" Grady reached for the bedroll tied behind his saddle.

"Sounds good to me." Trace dismounted and began gathering wood for a fire.

While the coffee boiled, the two men traded war stories. Grady had served as a Union spy while wearing a Confederate uniform. Sometimes his role was reversed and Trace began to think it didn't matter to Grady as long as it offered enough excitement.

Trace had seen his share of the carnage wrought on the battlefield. He had sustained two minor wounds but considered himself lucky to have survived.

"Since you're an old hand at this spy business, you probably have some ideas about how we should go about it."

"There's a couple of ways," Grady offered. "I can work directly with you, but the best bet would be to infiltrate one of the gangs. I've done some checking on the Barker boys, Ben Bickerstaff and Bob Lee. I'm sure you've heard of the shenanigans they've been up to."

"Yeah, there was some burning near Tyler. There's been some stuff in the papers. I was thinking I would mosey on up to Corsicana and try to get the lay of the land." Grady reached for the makin's and offered the sack to Trace.

As he rolled a quirly, Trace considered what Grady had proposed. "Could be a mite dangerous," he commented.

Grady did not reply immediately. When he spoke, his voice was grim. "Burdette, you might want to reconsider the Army's offer. I been in this business for a long time, and it's about as dangerous an occupation a man can get. You will be up against men who would kill you just for the fun of it."

He held up his hand before Trace could object. "Now, don't get all riled up. I know you went through the war, same as I did. I'm just trying to explain how this business works. You have a wife and she's expectin' ain't she? It's different with me. I'm not married and have no young ones. That is, that I'm aware of." He grinned showing even white teeth.

"I know the danger involved and I'm not new to having to kill a man. As for my wife, Anne understands the situation. What we need to do now is figure out a way to contact one another."

# CHAPTER NINE

T WILIGHT CAST ITS MUTED LIGHT over the land as Trace rode into Anderson. He dismounted in front of the doctor's office. No doubt the sawbones already knew about the yellow fever epidemic, but he might be unaware that there were cases in Brenham. The doctor's living quarters were separated from his office by a wide porch with an entrance into the house at both ends. Trace knocked on the office door although he knew the physician was probably at supper.

"Sorry to disturb you, Doc."

"Don't worry about that," the doctor replied holding open the office door.

"Is Mrs. Burdette all right? It's not time yet but . . ."

"It's not that Doc. It's about the yellow fever in Brenham. A couple of cases been reported. The army thought you should know about them."

"I know it's in Galveston but didn't know it had spread inland. I'd best order more medicines and get my supplies in order. Thank you for letting me know."

\* \* \*

John's face broke into a big grin when he saw Trace coming through the doorway. "Good to see you back in one piece. Annie, Annie, come greet your husband."

With a smile that matched her father's grin, Anne hesitated before walking toward Trace. He took her hand, kissed her cheek and held her in a loose embrace.

"I was worried. I'm so glad you had a safe trip."

77

"Yea, it all worked out. Are you alright?" Trace decided not to mention his meeting with Grady Hawkins. He would discuss it with John after Anne retired for the night.

"Oh, yes, I'm fine. Are you hungry? There's some fried chicken left from supper." Anne started toward the family quarters.

"Well, I'll admit I'm feeling kind a hollow. Had trail rations at noon."

"It will only take a few minutes. I'll call you when it's ready."

With Anne out of their hearing, Trace motioned John from behind the desk. The two men moved to the porch. "I don't want Anne to know this right now although she's bound to find out. There's two or three cases of yellow fever in Brenham."

"Oh, Lord! I read about the trouble in Galveston. It was bound to spread inland sooner or later." His face reflected his fear as he looked into the hotel.

"This could turn into a real bad time, Trace. You know Anne's not strong and with the baby and all . . ." John's voice choked up.

Trace nodded. "I'll do everything I can to keep her safe. Maybe she should go back home. The sickness spreads quicker where there's more people."

"Trace," Anne called from the lobby. "I have your supper ready."

\*   \*   \*

Anne retired to her bedroom. Settled in their chairs on the hotel porch, Trace built a cigarette while John filled his pipe. The men smoked in silence for a half dozen minutes. Trace discussed his meeting with Grady Hawkins. He explained how he met up with Grady and how the two men were going to work together.

John shook his head. "There aint' been much activity around here but plenty is going on elsewhere. Them two outlaws, Cullen Baker and Ben Bickerstaff, have been raising hell in a half dozen counties. They say Baker will kill a freedman on a trumped up charge for a few dollars. And Klan activity is picking up, too, although nobody will admit to seeing them."

"You got any idea who might be heading up the local Klanners?"

John turned to look at Trace, his expression grim. "I can't say for sure and got no proof at all."

"I understand that, John. I'd just like to have an idea who I'm up against."

"You can probably guess who most of them are. The die hards that won't admit the South lost and don't want the freed people to stay around here. It's a wonder they ain't done harm to the school or the teacher the way they have up around Marshall and over Galveston way. I try to tell Miss Mills she needs protection but she just smiles and says the Lord will protect her. But if she goes ahead with her plans to have school at night for the grownups, she's just asking for trouble."

"School at night,' Trace echoed.

"Yeah, she says the people who can't come in the daytime have just as much right to an education as the children."

"I think that young lady needs a good talking to. Not that I'm the one to do it but surely the Bureau agent would not approve of it."

"It depends on how much money he can spend. Makes him look good if he can report a goodly number of students. You know they pay a small fee and he gets to use it for the school." John knocked the ashes from his pipe and stood up. "I wish you luck, Trace. And you know I will help all I can. My worry is that Annie and the baby can be kept well and safe."

"Like I said, John. You know I'll do everything in my power to see that no harm comes to either of them."

\*     \*     \*

Heat waves danced in the distance as the hot Texas sun beat down on the dusty road. Regina looked down at the hem of her skirt and the boots she wore to protect her ankles from poisonous vegetation and possible snake bites. Most of her gowns were permanently stained even though the laundress who did the hotel's linens worked diligently to keep them looking clean and fresh.

Regina trudged toward the hotel, carrying the students' papers in a canvas bag. It had been a trying day. She was teaching the children their letters and most of them were having considerable difficulty. Granted, there were two children who seemed very bright. Brother and sister that Regina suspected had been given rudiments of reading and writing. Before the war it was illegal to teach Negroes to read and write; however, some plantations owners had allowed it. This was especially true if the children were the playmate of the owner's children, or personal body servants. She would have to spend the evening going over their papers and devising a way to simplify the lessons.

John watched as Regina entered the hotel. The young woman looked tired and her face appeared thinner than when she had come to Anderson. *She's not going to last. It's too much for a young lady with her gentile background.*

"Hello, Mr. Michaels." Her voice betrayed her weariness.

"Hello, Regina. How did it go today?"

"I will admit it is more difficult than I imagined, but the children are so eager to learn."

"Maybe so, Regina, but you must think of yourself. You're not used to the heat and I'm sure the schoolhouse is a far cry from the ones up north."

"That's true, but these children deserve an education. Some of the students I taught in Indiana didn't appreciate the opportunities they were given. And some of the parents didn't want to accept the fact that their children were not as intelligent as they thought they were."

Before John could reply, Anne came from the family quarters. "Oh, I didn't know you were home, Regina. You look tired. Why don't you lie down for awhile? Supper won't be ready for a good half hour."

Since Anne was staying at the hotel and preparing the meals, Regina had made arrangements to join them. She smiled. It was typical of Anne to be concerned about others and not dwell on her own problems. Her pregnancy was well advanced, but she continued to help her father with the hotel.

"Is there anything I can do to help you?" Regina asked.

"Thank you. The preparation is all done. It's just a matter of letting everything cook. Go on upstairs and rest. I'll call you when it's time to eat."

"Thank you. I am a bit tired." With a wan smile, Regina turned and climbed the stairs to her room. She opened the door and stepped inside. The curtains were drawn on the single window and the room was hot and stuffy. She opened the curtains and raised the window to let in fresh air. Regina had convinced Anne to let her do her own housekeeping. The bed was covered with a colorful quilt and the room was neat and orderly.

The rocking chair beckoned her to sit down and remove her boots. As she bent over to unhook the buttons, her eyes fastened on a sheet of paper lying in the middle of the bed. Had she overlooked a student's assignment? She was always careful to keep her materials in order. She abandoned unfastening her boots and removed the sheet of paper from the bed. Her eyes widened and the color left her face as she read the words printed in bold black letters.

**TEECHER GO HOME. YOU DON'T BELONG HEAR.**
**IF YOU DONT LEEVE YOU WILL BE KILT OR WURSE.**

Regina stared at the message. It was written on a sheet of ruled yellow paper. There were smudge marks and creases where it had been folded several times. The young woman's hands trembled as the words penetrated her brain. She knew there were people in Anderson who resented her, but that someone would do her physical harm was terrifying. What could she do? First, she would show the note to John Michaels. He was level headed and would know what to do.

As Regina turned to leave the room, she stumbled. Her legs felt weak and her body was trembling. She felt cold in spite of the heat. Sitting down on the edge of the bed, she tried to calm her racing heart by breathing deeply, resting between breaths. One of her boots was partly unhooked. Taking a deep breath she stood up and managed to pick up the button hook from where she had dropped it. It took her several tries before she refastened the buttons.

John Michaels was checking the register when Regina walked into the lobby. He looked up and the smile left his face in an instant. "Good Lord, woman, you look like you just seen a ghost!"

Regina tried to swallow the lump in her throat but it would not go down. Wordless, she handed him the note. He read the crude message and his expression hardened. "I been expecting something like this. Come, sit down and I'll have Annie bring you a cup of tea."

"Oh no, I don't want Anne to know anything about this. She would get upset and in her condition . . . ."

"I don't see how you can keep it from her. We should take this to the sheriff right away. And we need to let Trace know about it. This may be the break Trace is looking for."

Regina tried to relax and calm her racing emotions. Nothing like this had ever happened to her. The only unsettling experience she had when she was teaching in Indiana concerned one boy she caught cheating on a test. His father came to his rescue but his mother did not excuse him. He was reprimanded and nearly expelled. Due to Regina's persuasion, he was allowed to remain in school.

Anne called them to supper. Regina found she could not eat. The food seemed to stick in her throat. She could tell Anne was a bit puzzled. She was an excellent cook and Regina enjoyed the meals she prepared. "I'm sorry. I guess I'm overly tired tonight."

Anne smiled. "That's all right. I know teaching school here must be much harder than it was up north."

Regina tried to keep her voice from betraying her anxiety. "Yes, it is, but it's much more rewarding, too."

The meal finished, Anne rose and began clearing the table.

John and Regina exchanged glances. Something had to be done about the note. Trace was expected in town tomorrow morning. Perhaps they should wait and discuss the matter with him.

"Annie, I will help you with the dishes tonight. Regina should try to get some rest."

Turning to her friend Anne emphasized John's comment.

"Of course, Poppa. Her room should be a little cooler by now. And I will put on a kettle of water for your bath."

Regina smiled and hugged Anne. "You are true friends. I don't think I could stay in Texas without your friendship."

\*　　\*　　\*

Trace arrived early the next morning before Regina left for school. Anne was still in her bedroom, but Regina was dressed for the day. Her face was pale and her eyes were puffy. *She's still a mighty pretty woman.* Trace berated himself for having such thoughts. After all, he was a married man with a child on the way. No matter the child was not his. Anne was a wonderful young woman and deserved his complete attention. Attention? He was honest enough to admit he was not in love with Anne, but he did love her in a brotherly way.

"Do you want to show Trace the note?" John asked.

Regina opened her reticule and removed the folded missile. Without speaking, she handed it to Trace. He read the short message and his expression hardened. "It was lying in the middle of my bed when I returned from school yesterday afternoon."

"Has the sheriff seen this?", Trace questioned.

Regina shook her head. "No, we decided to show it to you first."

"I thought you would want to see it and the sheriff might not want you to know about it," John explained as he moved closer to Trace.

"Yeah, you know I'm still looking for that buckskin horse, among other things. But, the sheriff needs to know about it."

"Regina, if you want to go to his office I will be glad to escort you."

Regina, the fear still lingering in her eyes, nodded. "Yes, I know he should be informed, and I appreciate your offer to assist me."

Trace could not read the expression on the sheriff's face as he read the brief message. Did the man have any idea who might have written the note?

"This is not something new, Miss Mills. Other people who have been friendly toward the Negroes have received similar warnings."

"Do you think the same person or persons are sending all of them?" Trace asked.

The lawman shrugged. "Who knows? The writer either doesn't have much schooling or is deliberately misspelling them. The paper is from a plain school tablet." Turning to Regina, he asked, "When did you receive this?"

"Yesterday afternoon. I had just gotten home from school and went to my room to lie down for a while."

"And you usually dismiss the students around three or so?"

"Yes, the school room gets very uncomfortable in the afternoons."

"Do you walk home alone?"

"Why yes. There' never been any reason to be afraid."

"Until now, that is," Trace added, his voice hard.

# CHAPTER TEN

**T**WO DAYS LATER GRADY SHOWED up at the farm after dark. Trace was in the barn tending to a sick cow. She had gotten into a patch of locoweed and her milk could not be used. Trace did not hear Grady approach and grabbed for his revolver when a hand touched his shoulder.

"Easy Pard," Grady cautioned. "You don't want to antagonize a member of the Barker gang. We shoot first and ask questions later." His grin denied the threat.

Trace finished ministering to the cow and stood up. "There you are Flossie. You should feel a lot better in the morning." He gave her a pat on the rump, left the stall and latched it.

"Sounds like you met up with the Barkers."

Grady nodded. "I sure did. Cost me a month's pay but maybe I can get it back." He guffawed. "It's hard enough to get paid wages let alone reimbursed." Seeing the expression on Trace's face he hastened to add, "Don't worry, Burdette. Since you don't move around like I do, you probably won't have any trouble."

Trace shrugged. "Let's go in the house. I'll see if I can rustle us up some grub while you tell me what you've been up to."

After Anne's cold biscuits with butter and homemade jelly washed down with scalding hot coffee, Grady related how he came to meet up with the Barker gang. "I got into a poker game in Marshall. Pretty high stakes. I didn't try to win. Only a small pot now and then. The men were definitely hard cases. After a few drinks, their tongues kind a loosened up. They mentioned a couple of incidents but didn't say where they happened. Probably find out if we need to. I dropped a few hints about my 'past.' Told them I was looking for a way to get back at them damn Yankees and make some easy money."

Trace grinned. "About your background, I don't suppose you had to stray too far from the truth."

"I have had some experience on both sides. Anyway, I could tell they were interested. They didn't give out any information about their plans. I told them I had some unfinished business to take care of but I would be back in a few days. Now, you and me need to work out the details."

"I've been thinking on it and I may have a solution. There's not much work to do around here right now. Moses' grandson, Jimbo, might be able to bridge the gap between you and me, depending on where you are."

Grady scratched his head. "That will take some thought since I move around. I guess we could work out a central meeting place and leave some kind of messages. Let me think on it. Are you working on anything in this area?"

Trace drank the last of his coffee before answering. "I'm trying to get a lead on the *Klanners*. The new school teacher has been threatened." He related the incident involving the note and the sheriff's reaction.

"Maybe it's just as well you scout around here for awhile. Keep your ears and eyes open. Do you have any idea who might be involved?"

"Yeah, I have a suspicion. I patrol every night, a different area each time, but there hasn't been any activity. and I haven't given up finding that buckskin horse either. Something tells me it's not from around here."

Trace invited Grady to spend the night but he declined.

"I appreciate the offer, but I don't think that's a good idea. You never know who might be sneaking around and we don't want anybody to see us together. I plan to mosey on toward Marshall, then check out Corsicana and try to join up with Barker and his gang."

"I'll have a talk with Jimbo. We need to decide on the meeting place as soon as possible. There are a lot of abandoned homesteads that might work."

"If I find anything, I'll double back and let you know."

The two men shook hands and Grady vanished into the night.

\*　　\*　　\*

Moses and his grandsons were working in the barn when Trace came in to check on Flossie. "After we finish the chores, I want to have a talk with you."

The men looked at one another. *Was Massa Trace gonna let them go? There ain't much work and winter comin' on.*

Trace sensed their apprehension and knew he needed to quiet their fears. "Find a seat and I'll explain what I have in mind."

*   *   *

Anne rubbed her aching back. She had to give up climbing the stairs to clean the rooms. Regina tried to help but with her school work and lack of experience in domestic duties, the greater burden fell on Anne. Besides, Regina had been acting a bit strange lately. Something was a foot but Anne could not imagine what it was. She knew Regina did not want to give up her job and return home. *Oh, well, maybe it's my imagination. Everybody seems a little tense these days.*

Regina walked into the lobby, a frown marring her pretty features.

"Regina, is something wrong?"

"Oh, no. I was just thinking of the test I must administer. It is supposed to show the children's progress but . . . ," her voice trailed away.

"Don't worry so. I'm sure your pupils will make a good showing. After all, most of them have had no schooling at all."

"You're right, of course." With a wan smile, Regina climbed the stairs to her room.

Although there had been no further activity since the note, Regina could not shake the fear that something evil was lurking around the corner. She removed her outer clothing and stretched out on the bed. The heat in Texas was the only element she did not like. She smiled thinking of Nancy, her fastidious sister-in-law. Nancy would swoon if she could see how Regina ignored the wrinkled skirts and her untidy hair which seemed forever escaping its neat chignon.

*   *   *

John was behind the desk sorting mail into the cubbyholes. Several drummers used his address and picked up their mail when traveling the area. He looked up as Trace crossed the threshold. His manner more serious than Trace had ever seen it, he motioned to the back door.

When they reached the yard, John kept walking toward the creek that wound through the town. He stopped at the water's edge and turned to face Trace. "Doc told me there is a case of yellow fever at the Fanthrop Inn. Seems a man from Galveston stopped at the inn ailing. Miz Fanthrop called Doc and he recognized the symptoms. Miz Franthrop put him up and Doc said she told him she would nurse the man and keep ever'body away from him. He told me 'cause of Annie and said she should stay away from the stores and such. I haven't told her and don't know if I should."

Trace felt his gut lurch and his pallor was tinged with gray. Yellow fever! He should not be surprised because the epidemic was spreading. He thought of Annie and her condition. The baby was due in a month or so. How could he protect her from the devastating disease? "She's bound to find out sooner or later. Might as well be now so she can take precautions. Do you want me to tell her?"

John pursed his lips and finally answered. "Maybe we should both tell her. Regina should know, too so let's wait till after supper."

Trace nodded. When he thought of the gentle Anne in the throes of the terrible disease, a weight settled in his stomach and a deep pain clutched at his heart. Although he was not in love with Anne in the romantic sense, he loved her dearly as he would a favorite sister.

After supper they gathered in the family sitting room. The heat of the day lingered in the small space and Regina fanned herself with a folded newspaper.

"I'll make this quick," John said and explained the situation concerning the dreaded disease. "Annie," John warned his daughter, "I will do the shopping and all other chores that require going among the citizenry. Remember, you must do everything you can to protect yourself and the baby."

Both women had lost the color in their faces. Hands clasped tightly in her lap, Regina found her voice. "Does this mean that the school will be closed?"

John shook his head. "I don't know. I guess that would be up to Mr. Shields."

"But . . . but, I just had three women and one man asked me to teach night classes."

"That's out of the question, Regina," Trace responded, his voice firm.

Regina's face regained some of its color and her brown eyes narrowed. "Really, Mr. Burdette that is not your decision to make. Mr. Shields is in charge of this district and if he decides it is a good idea, then I am perfectly willing to teach the adults."

Trace grinned inwardly. *Little Miss Teacher is not as meek as she appears to be.* "Does he know about the note," he asked, his voice blunt.

"I don't know. I certainly didn't tell him. If he does, he may ask for my resignation. But, I'm not ready to give up."

"That's a Yankee for you. No, Regina, I don't think you're a quitter but there is such a thing as being foolhardy. You could be injured or worse." Trace liked the genteel woman but like most females, she lacked common sense.

Anne, who knew nothing about the note, stared at her father and Trace. "What note?" she asked.

*Now the fat is in the fire!* Trace glanced at Regina and John. "Might as well tell her," and he proceeded to reveal the story of the note.

Anne's face turned deathly white and she stared at Regina. "Oh, my, Regina, what are you going to do?"

"Go right on teaching. That's what I came here for."

"But, but . . . ," Anne was at a loss for words.

Trace rose and went to Anne's side. He put an arm around her shoulders. "Now don't fret, honey, you will be protected and so will Regina." Anne smiled at her husband. *Honey!* It was the first term of endearment he had ever said to her.

\* \* \*

Trace saddled Ulysses for his nightly ride. So far he had found no evidence of the Klanners and he was becoming discouraged. Although nothing unusual had happened around Anderson, violence was running rampant in the state. He led the horse from the barn and mounted up. For some reason he had been thinking about the Jacksons. Theirs was an idle farm as were many others in the area, but he had seen the brothers in the saloon more than once. Where did they get the money to buy liquor? His suspicions fully aroused, he turned Ulysess toward the east.

The area had become more overgrown since most of the farming had been abandoned. As Trace headed into the clump of trees and brush, he caught a faint whiff of smoke. Somebody was camped out. *Probably a bunch of renegades.* He dismounted and tied Ulysess to a stout branch.

He crouched down and made his way deeper into the woods. Suddenly, there was a sizeable clearing just ahead. The scene that greeted Trace chilled his blood. A fire was burning in the center of the clearing. That accounted for the smell of smoke. A group of men wearing hoods over their heads were gathered around something on the ground. Trace crept forward until he could see that it was a colored man.

"He ain't dead. Yet! Best we drop him off someplace where he can be easy found." The man who spoke was big and heavy set.

The voice was familiar but at the moment Trace could not remember where he heard it. The others nodded their heads and murmured their agreement. The hoods concealed their identity and he did not recognize any of them.

One of the men separated from the group and started walking in Trace's direction. *I'd better make tracks if I don't want to be caught.* The man left the path and Trace realized he was going for the horses. He glanced over his shoulder and saw the group going through some kind of ritual involving signs and low muttering. *Must be their secret code.* Trace increased his pace and hurried toward the place where he had tied Ulysess. He had to get word to Grady that the Klanners were working in the area.

*       *       *

Jimbo's cry roused Trace from a deep sleep. He had ridden hard to keep ahead of the Klanners. He had gone to bed a short time later after he reached the farm. Rufus was the colored man he saw at the meeting. He pulled on his britches and ran barefoot into the yard. Moses and Jimbo were squatting before a prostrate form lying on the ground.

"Massa Trace, it be Rufus. He hurt bad." Tears streamed down the old man' face. Jimbo's eyes filled but he struggled to hold back the tears.

Trace knelt to examine the boy's body. Just as he picked up Rufus hand, he opened his eyes and a faint smile touched his lips. "I . . . I . . . I be alright, Paw Paw." He looked at his grandfather, then shifted his gaze to Jimbo. He struggled to speak and blood gurgled from his lips. The light in his eyes began to fade. The faint smile settled on his face, he sighed and closed his eyes. Rufus was dead!

They buried Rufus under a giant oak tree that he favored. Colored folk were forbidden burial in the town's cemetery. Because of the epidemic, Anne did not attend the simple service Trace and Regina arranged. Several Negro families, including those of Regina's students, attended as did John, the sheriff and Joe Reynolds. Regina, being a devout Christian and the person with the most knowledge of the Bible read the eulogy she prepared with Moses help. Trace noted that her severe black gown made her features look as if they were carved out of ivory. Then he chastised himself thinking of Anne and their situation.

*The colored folks sang their spiritual songs and their voices mingled in the hot air. Although the slaves had been denied any semblance of Christianity, they had picked up remnants of the hymns and made them into their own versions.

Anne had prepared a meal and John and trace spread it out on a makeshift table near the house. After a respectable time, Trace, John, the sheriff and Joe left the crowd to mourn the loss of one of their own.

Trace, John, Sheriff Dawson and Joe Hutcheson sought out a shady spot where they could discuss Rufus' death.

The old man is pretty broken up over this," Trace told them. "Now Jimbo is all he has left of his family. We can't let the Klanners get away with all the destruction they are causing." Trace had told them of his patrols and the witness of Rusfus' fatal beating.

"Dammit, Burdette, we don't have a clue who is involved. We can't go around arresting innocent men."

Trace grinned although the gesture belied any humor. "I've got an idea or two, sheriff," he replied. ""But, like you say, I got no proof."

"You need to share all the information you got," Dawson's voice was hard.

Trace shook his head. "I said I have no proof and what was it you said about innocent people?"

The sheriff's face colored up. "Said we couldn't arrest them without proof but we can still pull them in for questioning."

Again, Trace shook his head. "No, if they are guilty, that would just tip them off." Grady could have hooked up with the Klanners. He had not mentioned Grady to anyone and wanted to keep it that way.

"There haven't been any strangers around the hotel," John volunteered.

Joe Hutcheson laughed. "I don't think it's strangers we have to worry about. It's our friends and neighbors we have to watch.'

"And don't forget those roaming outlaws like the Barkers and Jacksons. They're raisin' hell up around Marshall and Corsicana but that don't mean they can't ride down here." Trace reminded them.

• Gospel hymns are time and are not bound by the constraints of a single lifetime. The faith that inspired these songs, that guided the poets and hymn writers of days gone by, lives from generation to generation, proclaiming that God IS. And that the world truly is in His hands.

The above is from the book *Amazing Grace, a country salute to great gospel hymns*, written by J. Countryman and published by The Thomas Nelson Book Group; copyright 2005

# CHAPTER ELEVEN

"**I**F YOU WILL EXCUSE ME, I must get back to the school house," Regina said, rising from her seat at the supper table.

"Regina," John spoke up, "are you sure you need to teach the adult classes at night? You know I will be glad to escort you to the school and back, but it could still be dangerous."

"I feel obligated to teach the adults who really want to learn. As you know, they have never had the advantage before through no fault of their own. Most of them cannot attend school in the daytime. I shall be extremely watchful."

"I pray you don't have any trouble," Anne joined in.

"Thank you," Regina smiled at Anne. *She does not look good. She's pale and aside from her pregnancy she is too thin. I wonder if Trace realizes how frail she is?* "Let me get my shawl and supplies and we can be on our way."

When Regina and John arrived at the school house, they found four women and two men waiting for her. Regina was delighted to see them and quickly unlocked the door. "Come in," she urged them forward. "Take any seat you like. It will be yours from now on. I'm sure you all know my name, but in case you are new in this area, I am Regina Mills and I will be your teacher."

John took a seat at the back of the room and made himself comfortable. He was going to stay until the class was over and escort Regina back to the hotel.

"We will do a little work tonight, but first I need to ask your names so that I can make up a grade book. Let's start with the ladies first."

The women looked at each other. Ladies? They had never been called a lady in their lives. A buxom young woman in the first row spoke up. "My name is Edna Johnson."

This was followed by a much older woman named Fannie Taylor, a very pregnant young woman, Maggie Clark ; and Alice Sanders.

Then it was the men, both young, spoke in a soft drawl.

"Us'ns is the Davis twins. I'm Aaron and this is my brother Handy."

Six black shining faces stared back at her, and Regina noted they were all scrubbed and wore clean clothing. She finished writing their names in her grade book with brief side notes to identify them.

"Perhaps some of you have a little knowledge of the alphabet and we will start by learning the letters." She held a stack of cards in her hands with each letter printed on it. She held up the first one. "This is the letter 'A'. A word that starts with the letter A is apple."

John watched with interest as Regina covered half of the alphabet. The students, their eyes wide with wonder, hung on every word. She had passed out paper and pencils and asked the students to copy the letters as she identified them. Each letter was given a word to illustrate how it was used. "Don't try to copy the word," Regina told them. "Just concentrate on learning to write the letter."

John took his watch from his pocket and saw that Regina had been teaching for an hour.

She had told him that the first class would be a short one.

He caught her glance and pointed to his watch.

"Are there any questions," she asked. The students shook their heads in unison. Regina knew questions would come later.

"If not, then I think we have covered enough for tonight. Practice learning the letters we studied tonight and tomorrow night we will take up the rest of the alphabet. Class dismissed."

"I think it went very well, don't you" Regina asked John as they walked through the darkness.

"Yes, it did. You are a fine teacher, Regina."

"Thank you, John. I love my work and want to continue teaching as long as I can."

\*     \*     \*

The shadows and shapes formed by the darkness swirled around Trace as he guided Ulysess on the narrow path. He didn't know where it led. It was far from his farm and familiar landmarks. There had been no acts of violence in the area since Rufus was killed, but several incidents had occurred near Marshall and Corsicana. A school had been burned as well as a Negro church. Its pastor had been warned not to preach again or he would be preaching in hell.

Trace decided to head in that direction. He hoped to meet up with Grady but it was not likely. They had not found a meeting place. Trace was afraid to send Jimbo to find him after Rufus's death. Moses could not take another loss in his family.

Ulysess snorted and shook his head. A large object loomed up in the darkness, directly in Trace's path It was a building. Several yards away there were skeletal remains of a farmhouse. Trace concentrated on the single building. He dismounted and looped the reins over a nearby branch. Drawing his revolver, he crept forward. There were no horses in sight but Trace knew the building could conceal several men. Keeping to the shadows and crouching low, Trace approached the structure. It was not big or tall enough to be a barn. There were no windows and Trace guessed it had been some kind of utility building The door was open and hanging by one hinge. He had heard no sound since he came upon the place. He stepped inside and caught the faint odor of wood smoke. It had been a smoke house where hams, bacon and sausage were cured and kept. There were no other structures nearby, but Trace could see skeletal remains several yards away.

Little feet made scurrying sounds as Trace walked forward. Mice! Evidently the place had been abandoned for a long time. He struck a match and saw the shelves on the wall had been ripped off. The fire pit was filled with ashes and small pieces of half burned wood, all encased by an elaborate design of spider webs. The dirt floor showed no sign of human tracks. It would make an ideal meeting place. *Now, if I can just get word to Grady.*

Trace cut a branch from one of the trees surrounding the building and wiped his tracks from the floor of the building. No use advertising that somebody had discovered the abandoned place. He was still puzzling over how he was going to reach Grady when he heard the sound of approaching hoof beats. He led Ulysess into the brush and waited. There were three riders and they wore hoods over their heads. From the meager light of the quarter moon, Trace could barely make out the color of the horses and their markings. His eyes fastened on the leader riding in front of the single file. The horse was a buckskin!

"Well boys, another mission completed."

The voice sounded familiar but Trace could not place it.

"Yeah," one of the riders picked up the conversation. "Did you see how that ol' black boy tried to defend the girl? Good thing we was holdin' him while you was . . . a . . . . pokin' her."

"I don't think there will be any trouble out of them. We could have strung them up, you know. This way they'll serve as a warning to them black devils. My guess is that they will light out of these parts real quick like."

The riders did not stop at the abandon smoke house but continued on in a north westerly direction. Their voices died away and Trace considered following them. Maybe they would lead him to Grady. He hesitated. He was already a long way from home and if he started back, it would be dawn before he arrived. Even if the scout was in the outlaw camp, it would be difficult to draw his attention without being discovered. Trace turned Ulysess toward home.

*   *   *

The second adult class brought another man to Regina's classroom. He was a few years older than the twins. "Welcome to the class," Regina began. "I am Miss Mills. May I have your name, please?"

"Ben O'Connor."

"Please take a seat, Mr. O'Connor. It will be yours for the remainder of the class."

*O'Connor? That's quite unusual. It must have been the name of his master.*

Regina began reviewing the letters she had taught the students the night before. "Who can tell me the letters we learned last evening?" She held up the letter 'H'.

The silence was deafening. Regina smiled. "Don't be bashful. You all want to learn and this is the way to begin." She held the card a little higher.

"That's an 'H'," Ben O'Connor volunteered.

"Yes it is, but tell me Mr. O'Connor, how do you know that? You were not here last evening."

The young man smiled and answered "I know my letters ma'am. I can read some, too. Mr. Patrick taught me how."

Regina's eyes widened. My goodness! He must have had an understanding master who was not afraid of the authorities. "That's wonderful Mr. O'Connor. Perhaps you would like to assist me when I work individually with the class?"

"I would be honored, ma'am and please call me Ben."

After Ben identified the letter, Regina went on and was surprised that several of the students gave correct answers. Regina's eye misted ever so slightly. How could the powers that be deny these people even the most basic human rights.

Maggie Clark raised her hand. "May I be excused, ma'am? I'm feeling poorly."

"Yes, of course, Maggie. Do you need help getting home?"

The pregnant woman's pallor was a grayish black and she, indeed, did not look well. "No, ma'am. My man is waiting outside fur me."

"I hope you feel better soon. If there's anything I can do, please let me know."

The woman rose heavily to her feet and shuffled from the room. There was a minute of silence, then the older woman whispered, "She gonna loose that youngun, sure as my name is Edna Johnson."

Regina covered the remainder of the alphabet and had the students practice the letters. "Tomorrow evening we will put both parts of the alphabet together and commit them to memory. They are the basis for everything you will learn." She gave several examples of the letters and the words they began with. The students were attentive and their faces reflected their enthusiasm.

When Regina joined John in the school yard, she felt a sudden chill. "John, where are you?"

"I'm right here." He was sitting on a bench that had been placed under s big live oak tree. "I'm OK. Just got a little stuffy in the school house. Are you all right?"

Regina pulled her shawl tighter around her shoulders. She did not know why she felt unsettled and a little nervous. "I'm just tired. Although I love the teaching, two classes in one day are tiring."

"Maybe you should cut the classes to three a week instead of four."

"No, I would rather not do that. The students have so little opportunities as it is. Besides, who knows how long the classes will last? There may not be enough money for long. And, heaven forbid, the outlaws could cause trouble at any time." Regina shivered although it was a balmy evening with only a gentle breeze to disturb the stillness. The shadows mingled with the light from the pale moon and seemed to move from place to place. Regina felt uneasy but did not want to alarm John.

They reached the hotel and found Anne in their quarters asleep on the sofa. The harried look and worry lines in her face were smoothed out. She was relaxed, her breathing deep and even. "She looks like an angel," John whispered.

"She is," Regina replied. "I've never known anyone like her. So kind and caring."

"She takes after her mother,. My Maureen was the soul of compassion. She never refused to help out when it was needed. And sometimes when it wasn't," John chuckled. "Yes, my girls have been a great blessing. The Good Lord is taking care of my Maureen in heaven and I do my best here on earth to take care of Annie."

For some unexplained reason, Regina felt that shiver run down her spine. *What is wrong with me? I am acting like an old maid school teacher afraid of her own shadow. I must pull myself together. I don't want John and Anne worrying about me. I am afraid for Anne and the baby, but I can't let John know.*

*       *       *

Trace arrived at the farm as dawn was streaking the sky. Moses and Jimbo were fast asleep in their little room off the barn. He unsaddled Ulysess and rubbed him down. The horse had been ridden long and hard and deserved a ration of oats. Trace patted the grey gelding on the neck "I made a good choice when I picked you, old boy."

The water bucket on the porch was empty and Trace filled it from the well. He splashed cold water on his face, dried on it on a scrap of cloth hanging on a nail, and went into the house. The \stove was cold and he thought about building a fire and cooking some breakfast, but he was tired from the long ride. Since Ann was staying in town, Trace had been using the bedroom. It was reminiscent of Anne with some of her belongings there and the faint scent of rose water lingered in the air. Anne! *It won't be long until the baby comes. I hope and pray she doesn't come down with the fever. She would never survive it, she is so small and weak.* He fell asleep with a silent prayer that Anne would come through the delivery all right and that the baby would be healthy.

"Now, you gonna wake Massa Trace with all that wood choppin',. Moses chastised Jimbo. "He didn' come home till most daylight an' he be mighty tired."

Trace heard the axe hitting the wood and turned over on his back. He had barely pulled off his pants and was still wearing his shirt and socks. His eyes roamed over the room and all the little touches of Anne that remained. He smiled remembering her kind and gentle spirit. *Maybe after the baby comes we can have a real marriage.*

Trace awoke when the sun was descending toward the west. He wanted to ride into town to see Anne. He rose and not taking time to heat the water, shaved his face clean of three days worth of whiskers. A change of clothes was in order, and he found them ironed and neatly folded in a chest that Anne had brought to the farm. A trip to the creek was a treat he thoroughly enjoyed. Splashing and ducking his head under, he soaped himself liberally with a bar he had found in the chest.

When Trace returned to the house, he found Moses and Jimbo in the kitchen. Moses was slicing bacon and Jimbo carrying the coffee pot to the stove. "Cain't make no biscuits Massa Trace, but I can fry up some corn pone."

"That will do just fine, Moses. After supper, I'm going to ride into town to see Miss Anne."

"I'se hope she be alright." That was the closet Moses could come to referring to Anne's condition.

"I'm sure she is. John and Regina are taking good care of her."

*   *   *

A scream split the night air. Trace halted Ulysess and listened. The sound seemed to come from the direction of the school house. He spurred the gelding and saw three figures in what looked like some kind of confrontation. Just then the moon came from behind a cloud and he recognized Regina's upturned face. Her eyes were wide with fright and she was struggling with one of the assailants while the other one was occupied with the other man.

Trace was off his horse and flung the man away from Regina. She stumbled and fell to her knees. She was sobbing softly but Trace had no time to see to her. He tried to pull the hood from the man's face but it slipped through his fingers. The other pair were punching and hitting and grunts of pain punctuated the air. With a lucky punch, the hooded man downed his opponent. He ran to the horses tied nearby. He mounted and rode the animal right up to Trace and the struggling assailant.

""This fracas is over. Throw down your gun, Burdette." His revolver was trained on Regina who had managed to get to her feet. Trace pitched his weapon in the dirt. The outlaw motioned with his head. "Come on. Let's get out of here."

Trace knew he could not follow them with Regina suffering from shock. The man who had been trying to defend her came up to them, brushing the dirt from his clothes. Trace was startled to see he was a Negro with light skin.

"Ben, did they hurt you? Oh, Trace this is Ben O'Conner. He is one of my adult students. John had to stay with Anne and Ben offered to walk me home. Ben, this is Trace Burdette, a good friend of John's." Regina knew she was babbling but she couldn't seem to stop.

The two men shook hands. "I'm sorry Miss Mills that I could not hold those men off."

"My goodness, Ben. There were two of them."

Trace took charge. "You've had a bad time, Regina. We'd best get you home."

# CHAPTER TWELVE

A SOON AS TRACE HAD seen Regina safely back to the hotel, he went looking for the sheriff. He found Dawson in the Ace High Saloon. The lawman was leaning against the bar but there was no drink in his hand. "Could I have a word with you, Sheriff?"

Dawson straightened up and seeing the expression on Trace's face, motioned toward the door. "Let's go to my office."

There was no conversation as they walked. The lawman unlocked the door and Trace saw a low light burning in the cell block which was devoid of prisoners. Dawson sat in the chair behind the desk. "I have a hunch you have something bad to tell me. Pull up a chair."

Trace related what had happened to Regina. "She has been warned but she won't give up and go back home. Stubborn woman!"

The sheriff grinned in spite of himself. "She's got grit, I'll give her that. But there's some foolishness there, too. A white woman walking with a Negro man at that time of night could cause all kinds of talk. This ain't Indiana, you know. Now, did you recognize either of them?"

"No. They had hoods over their heads."

"Well, we can't track them in the dark. I'll mosey on over there at first light and see if I can pick up some sign."

\*   \*   \*

Regina tried to down play the incident in order to keep it from Anne. She had gone to her room as soon as it was feasible. Sleep was elusive and she kept seeing and feeling the two men as they struggled to subdue her. Thank God for Trace! She shivered and pulled the quilt up to her chin. Perhaps I should go back to Indiana. Then she thought of David, her brother, and his objections for making the trip. Oh, how he would chastise her and remind her of his warnings. No! She would not run back home like a scared child. No harm was done and she would be more careful in the future. Besides, Anne needed her. She couldn't leave her to face the baby's birth without a woman friend to help her.

Regina fell asleep to be troubled by disjointed dreams of the attack and the cry of a newborn baby. Anne was weeping as was John and Trace' eyes were misty. The dream faded and Regina came awake with a start. The sunshine was peaking through her bedroom windows. *Good heavens I'm going to be late for school.*

Trace was gone when Anne and Regina went down for breakfast. Regina took time to drink a cup of coffee and eat one of the biscuits John took from the oven. As she hurried off to school, John cautioned her. "Regina, I will go to see Mr. Shields this morning if you want me to. I'm sure he will want to look into the matter."

"Yes, it will be all right for you to do that, John. But, I doubt it will come to anything. It was dark and the . . . the culprits were not recognized. I'll keep a careful watch for anyone who looks suspicious."

"If you are bound and determined to teach your night class, Trace will escort you home."

"Oh, yes, I want to continue with the classes. The students are so eager to learn."

*     *     *

It was imperative that Trace find Grady. For some reason, he had a hunch Grady knew about the abandoned smoke house. It was risky to go there in the day time, but he had to take the chance. It was nearing noon when he spotted the building in the overgrown brush. He rode off the trail in the opposite direction and hid Ulysess among the trees. Crouching low, he approached the building. He heard no noise except that of birds and scurrying wild life. There were no horse droppings, fresh or otherwise. Trace looked inside the smoke house and it appeared to be just as he had left it. Trace decided to follow the trail a little farther. The brush grew thicker. Ulysess snorted as if to say where in the world are we going? Trace laid a hand on the horse's neck and whispered, "Easy boy, easy."

The brush began to thin out. Trace dismounted and led Ulysses off the trail. The trail disappeared and a clearing lay ahead. There was a large corral and Trace estimated it held about fifteen head of horses. Some were milling around while others stood hip shot as if boredom had gotten the best of them. The dust cleared enough for Trace to look over the herd. His heart hit his stomach. A big buckskin horse appeared and Trace recognized it was the one who helped destroyed his cotton patch. His gut instinct told him there had to be somebody guarding the horses. Just then a man appeared at the opposite side of the corral. *Grady!* Well, *Ill be damned!* There could be others. Trace decided to wait and watch until he was sure Grady was alone. He had to be careful that Grady didn't mistake him for the enemy. After what seemed an eternity, Trace decided Grady was alone. How to get his attention without getting shot? It was a risk he had to take.

"Grady! Grady Hawkins. It's Trace Burdette."

Grady whirled around, his pistol appearing in his hand like magic. "Drop your gun and show yourself."

Trace stepped out of the brush, hands in the air. Grady grinned and holstered his weapon. "Well, you old horse thief. You plan on taking the herd all by yourself?"

"No, just that buckskin. He's the one who helped ruin my cotton crop. Have any idea who rides him?"

"Yep. Fellar by the name of Jackson. He's a mean son of a bitch."

"Which one? One of them is missing a leg. Complements of a Union mine ball."

"Nsw. It's the other one. Think his name is Joe. Let's get out of sight. There's a camp back in the woods, and I'll fill you in on what's been going on."

The campsite was far back in the woods where a small stream ran slow and easy. It looked as if it wasn't used very often with nothing but a coffee pot hanging over the fire pit. There were a few pieces of gear here and there. "All the comforts of home," Grady explained as he waved a hand around the camp. His bedroll was neatly tied and placed under a big live oak tree. "I can make us a pot of coffee," he volunteered.

"That sounds good, Trace responded. "Do you expect *visitors* anyways soon?"

Grady shook his head. "aw, they come in after dark and leave 'fore daylight. These horses are the ones they use on their raids. 'Fraid their regular ones might be recognized."

"Wonder where they got so many head?"

"Probably stole 'em from farms and ranches in West Texas. Take a look at the brands. Not many horses left around these parts." Grady busied himself with making the coffee using water from the stream.

"Mind if I take a look around?" Trace wanted to memorize the place in the event he made another trip to the area.

Grady grinned. "Not much to see but help yourself."

As Grady had told him, there wasn't much to see. Just lots of trees and brush. Evidently the outlaws used the camp as a stopping off place and kept their horses here. Now that Trace knew the identity of the buckskin's owner, he could keep an eye on the Jackson place. It would be interesting to see who showed up there.

"Well, pard," Grady interrupted Trace's thoughts. "We could use the old smoke house as a meeting place. There are plenty of places to hides messages if we need to."

"Sounds like a good idea. But I may not be doing much since the baby is due real soon. I want to stick close to home. I will check out the Jackson place and if anything comes up, I'll get word to you."

Grady grinned. "Yeah, I keep forgetting you're going to be a *daddy* real soon."

A faint flush stained Trace's neck and face. *Yes, I will be a father to the baby. It's the least I can do for Anne and Alvin.*

"By the way, since you want to stick close to home, I'll ride to Brenham and turn in a report. Might even be able to pick up some back pay."

"That would sure be welcome," Trace replied.

With promises to keep each other informed, the two men shook hands and Trace headed for home.

Twilight was upon the land when Trace arrived in Anderson. The sun slid below the horizon, and the shadows began to make their appearance. Trace thought of Regina and the previous night's trouble. He wondered if she was at the school house and decided to ride by and check it out. The lamps were burning inside the building and he knew Regina was involved with her students. He did not want to disturb her. The less the students knew, the better.

John was in the lobby when Trace walked into the hotel. From the look on John's face, he knew something was not right. "Anne?" His voice was hoarse and his stomach knotted up. "Now, don't worry. She's just feeling a little poorly. The preacher's wife is with her."

"Would it be alright if I go see her?"

"Of course. You're her husband and she needs comforting."

Anne was propped up in bed, numerous pillows supporting her back. Her skin was pale and had a waxy look to it. Her eyes lit up and she smiled when Trace came to the bedside.

"I have been waiting for you to have supper with me. Would you mind eating in here? Mrs. Foster refuses to let me get out of bed."

Trace hurried to the bedside and placed a tender kiss on her forehead. She was so fragile, and she looked like an angel in her white lace-trimmed nightgown. "I would be honored, Mrs. Burdette."

Trace shared a meal of succulent roast beef, oven browned potatoes and died apple pie.

He noticed that Anne barely touched her food. "You're a mighty find cook, Mrs. Foster."

The preacher's wife blushed like a young girl. "Why thank you Mr. Burdette. My husband keeps telling me so."

"And he's right." Turning to Anne, he asked, "Anne, is there anything you need,?"

""Not that I know of. Mrs. Foster is taking very good care of me."

"I'm in your debt, ma'am."

"Not at all Mr. Burdette. The Reverend is coming by later to see Anne and escort me home. If you would like to have your after dinner smoke downstairs, I'm sure Anne won't mind."

"Thank you, ma'am." Trace placed his arm around Anne's shoulder and squeezed gently. He followed the hug with a soft brush of his lips against hers. "Goodnight, sweetheart. Sleep well." *Now where did that come from?*

When Trace reached the lobby, John was talking with a man he did not recognize.

The man was past his prime. He was clean but his clothes had seen many wash tubs. His brown eyes were clear and direct.

"Trace, this is Mr. Stubbens. He says that two more people have died of the fever. My son-in-law, Trace Burdette."

The old man's handshake was firm. "Yes, sir," he said. "One of the ones who passed was a Negro but the other was a white woman. This fever thing is getting out of control but there don't seem much we can do about it."

"No," Trace agreed. "Just take all the precautions you can and stay close to home."

The man took his leave and Trace and John moved to the porch. "This fever worries me, Trace. Annie is so . . . so delicate and in her condition . . ."

"It worries me too, John. By keeping her confined to the hotel, maybe she will not come in contact with it."

"I pray to God you're right. I think it's time to walk Regina home. I can go if you want to stay with Annie."

"She needs her rest. I'll fetch Regina home."

*     *     *

Regina had just dismissed the class when Trace arrived at the school house. The students came out of the building talking in low tones. No doubt they had heard of the incident involving Regina.

"She a brave one, awright.," an older woman spoke up.

At that point, Ben O'Conner joined the others. Seeing Trace, he left the group and approached Trace. "Good evening, Mr. Burdette."

Trace nodded. "O'Connor.," he acknowledged.

"I feel bad about last night. I offered to take Miss Mills class tonight but she wouldn't hear of it."

"That's Regina for you. As stubborn as an Indiana mule." Trace caught Regina's stare. Her mouth tightened and Trace saw the anger in her expression. He grinned to show he was only joshing and the anger disappeared as swiftly as it came. There was little conversation as Trace and Regina walked to the hotel. Regina inquired about Anne, and Trace said she was not feeling well.

"Is there anything I can do.?"

"The preacher's wife was there when I left." Trace related the details of the supper he had shared with Anne.

"That was very thoughtful of you. I know Anne appreciated it."

Trace made no reply and they walked on in silence. When they reached the place Regina had been attacked, Trace could feel her shudder and he took her hand. "It's over. They won't try this spot again." Regina did not reply but tightened her hold on his hand.

*He's a strong man. Anne is lucky to have such a good husband.*

The couple reached the hotel, and after thanking Trace for seeing her home Regina went to her room. She was tired and for some reason felt nervous and jittery. It's because of the attack. Not because Trace was holding her hand, but she could still feel the work-hardened calluses and the strength in his fingers. Regina Louise Mills! *Hes your best friend's husband.* And Annw was ill and about to deliver a baby. She should be ashamed of ashamed of herself. And she was.

*   *   *

Anne was not well enough to come to the breakfast table. Regina, with John's help, prepared a tray and took it upstairs. She put on a bright smile, but inwardly she was shocked at the change in Anne's appearance. Her face was pale and her skin had a grayish tint. Her dark brown eyes seemed to swallow up her countenance. "Good morning." Regina placed the tray on the bedside table. "Would you like to freshen up a bit?"

"Yes, that would be lovely."

Regina poured water into the basin on the dresser. She wet a wash cloth and took it to Anne who began to wash her face. "I must look a fright."

Regina shook her head. "No, you are a lovely young women and once the baby comes, you will blossom again." She busied herself with trying to make Anne more comfortable.

Anne made a feeble attempt to taste the fluffy scrambled eggs and buttered toast. "Has Trace come in yet?" Anne knew Trace rode at night trying to find evidence of the Klan. He never talked about his work but Anne knew it was dangerous.

"I don't think so." Regina answered. "Is there anything I can get you?"

"Not really. I just can't get comfortable. I have an idea the baby is about to make his or her appearance soon."

"If you're sure there is nothing I can do, I'll take the tray back to the kitchen. Then I must get ready for school." Regina kissed Anne on the cheek and smoothed her hair before picking up the tray. "I'll help you brush your hair when I get home. That is, if you'd like."

"Oh yes. That would be a real treat."

When Regina entered the kitchen, she noticed that Trace was not there. *Oh my. I hope nothing has happened to him. Anne would be devastated.*

*   *   *

Trace had watched the Jackson farm the better part of the night. There had been no activity. The place remained dark and silent. Dawn was not far away and he did not want to get caught by the Jackson brothers. He rounded up Uylsess and, tightening the cinch, swung into the saddle. It was high time he went home to his wife. Anxiety about her condition and the yellow fever epidemic had his nerves on edge. He pushed Ulysess since the gelding had rested all night.

When he reached the hotel, he went straight to Anne's room. She was sleeping, her light breathing hardly stirring the covers. Her face, relaxed in sleep, mirrored the exhaustion that claimed her. The dark shadows around her eyes were tinged with purple. He touched her cheek and felt the heat. Not wanting to wake her, he went in search of John.

He found John in the kitchen having a cup of coffee. Trace got right to the point. "John I think we should `get the doctor to look in on Anne. She's running a fever and her color is bad."

John nodded. "I was thinking the same thing."

"Also. we need a woman to care for her, It's too much to expect from Regina with her school and all. It shouldn't be too hard to find someone. Maybe the Doc might know somebody. As soon as I grab a bite to eat, I'll get busy."

*   *   *

The doctor came within the hour, followed by a buxom Negro woman. He went directly to Anne's room. As he climbed the stairs, he said, "This is Maybelle. She is willing to look after Miss Anne." He motioned the woman to follow him.

After what seemed an eternity, the doctor came into the lobby where Trace and John were waiting. He shook his head. "I'm not sure about it, but . . . but she may have caught the fever."

Trace felt like he had been hit in the gut and John's normally ruddy complexion went stark white.

"Are you sure, Doc?" Trace' voice was tinged with emotion.

"No, but if her condition worsens . . ."

"The baby?" John's cheeks were wet with tears.

"It's hard to tell. We'll just have to wait and see."

107

# CHAPTER THIRTEEN

ANNE TRIED TO SIT UP but it was an impossible task. Her strength was waning more and more each day. She knew in her heart that she may not recover from the birth. The thought deepened her sadness that she might never see her precious baby. But another thought crept into her mind. If she died, she would be with Alvin again. She smiled. The thoughts were bittersweet. She was not sure which she preferred because she was so tired and weary.

"Miz Anne, you gotta eat more. Your little baby need nourishment." Maybelle, who had arrived in time to bring Anne her breakfast frowned at the barely touched tray.

"I'm not hungry," Anne replied.

Maybelle shook her head. "Maybe a nice warm bath would help. You up to it?"

"Oh, yes, that would be nice."

Regina knocked on the door before stepping into the room. "Good morning, Anne. Good morning Maybelle. How are you feeling Anne?"

Anne tried her best to act cheerful but it was an effort that Regina saw through. "I slept fairly well last night."

"That's good. You need your rest. Is there anything I can get for you? Anything you need?"

"I don't think so. Maybelle has offered to help me with a bath."

"That would be lovely. I know it will make you feel better." She squeezed Anne's hand. "I have to be on my way."

\*　　\*　　\*

Trace knew he had to contact Grady and headed for the old smoke house. It was slow going in the dark and Ulysess picked his way carefully through the tall grass. Trace reached his destination before dawn. There was a note in the place that he and Grady had chosen to hide their communications. By the light of several concealed matches, he read Grady's scrawled handwriting.

*Planning a big raid before dawn on Sunday. They still don't trust me so I'll be staying behind. If you can get here early enough, you might be able to identify some of them. I think they are planning to hit the Corsicana area.*

The note was unsigned.

If he interpreted the note correctly the raid would be pulled off in the wee hours of tomorrow since it was now Saturday night. As much as he hated to leave Anne, Trace needed to learn the identity of the Klan. He knew the Jackson brothers were mixed up in the activities but there were others. He needed to get names and dates of possible additional raids. He mounted the grey gelding and rode toward the outlaw horse corral.

The night was dark and quiet. Nocturnal creatures were about but Trace took little note of them. His mind was on Anne and her condition. He had never voiced his thoughts to anyone, but Trace had a bad feeling about the situation. Anne was so young and fragile and the pregnancy coupled with the deep grief of Alvin's death took its toll. He did not like to think about either Anne or the child succumbing to the fever, but he knew it was a definite possibility.

He forced the dark thoughts from his mind and continued on.

The vegetation began to thin out and Trace knew he was nearing his destination. He needed to get off the trail and find a hiding place. The light from a huge fire nearly blinded him and he knew he should back away. If he was caught, they would hang him on the spot. He decided to use two giant oak trees as his cover. There was a space between them and he hunkered down to wait.

The riders arrived by twos and threes until Trace counted nine of them. It was difficult to distinguish their features but he dared not move closer. The riders turned their mounts into the corral. Trace caught a glimpse of Grady, riding bareback, cutting animals out of the herd. The men settled around the fire talking quietly among themselves. Suddenly, a tall man arose and stepped between the fire and the riders. His voice sounded familiar and when he turned in Trace's direction, Trace recognized Fred Collins. He had been at the stage depot when Trace arrived in Anderson. Also, he had been Trace's father's best friend. The Jackson brothers were there as was Williams who had refused to sell Trace a cow and chickens.

Collins spoke. "It's time to ride. Cullen will be waiting for us at the church." In a flurry of activity the men caught up their mounts, Before mounting his hose, Collins spoke to Grady but kept his voice low and Trace could not distinguish the words. Hoods appeared on the heads of the men and they were off in a cloud of dust.

Trace waited until he was sure the men at left. He came out of his hiding place and joined Grady who was rounding up the horses the Klaners had ridden to the rendezvous. After quieting them down, he offered them a forkful of hay and a small ration of oats.

"Do you think we should follow them? I could try to warn the people. Ulysses' is pretty fast." Trace volunteered.

"Naw, they outnumber us too much. I think they are headed southwest of Corsicana. There is a Negro church at the cross roads. It has quite a few members and the preacher is not afraid to give them Klaners hell. They been threatening to burn them out for qute awhile. I guess they finally decided to do it."

"The next time they plan something like this, we have to try and catch them. We have to warn the sheriff. I'll clue him in on the ones that were here tonight. He can get up a posse. They have to be stopped!"

\*     \*     \*

When Trace returned to Anderson, the hotel was ablaze with light. "Every lamp in the place must be lit." He took the stairs two at a time and when he reached Anne's room, he found Regina and John sitting in the hall. The door was closed and Trace heard the mummer of low voices but could not make out the words.

John came to his feet and Regina followed. "The doctor is with her. And Maybelle."

"It don't look good, Trace."

Trace's ruddy complexion turned pale and he stripped of his jacket. He went to the door and knocked softly. Maybelle answered and looking at the doctor, motioned him inside.

"I won't lie to you, Trace. Anne is very weak and we could lose both of them."

"Her contractions are coming faster now and she doesn't have the strength to push the baby out. I'm going to try to help her but I think you should try to comfort John. He's in bad shape."

Trace walked to the bedside and looked down at his wife. Her sin was as white and smooth as alabaster. Her brown eyes were wide in her small face. And Trace saw a glimmer of tears. He knelt by her side and placed his hand on her forehead. It was cold and clammy. "It's going to be all right, Anne. The doctor and Maybelle are right here and they are going to help you. We will have a son or daughter in a little while".

Anne tried to smile but Trace could tell the pain was nearly unbearable. He took her small hand in his and squeezed it gently. Leaning over he whispered for her ears only, "I love you, Anne."

Her face underwent a transformation. Her smile seemed as bright as the candles in the room. "Take care of my baby, Trace."

"I will. You know I will."

The doctor frowned, "Trace, I think you had better let Anne get some rest now. We still have a way to go.'"

In the dark before the dawn, a thin wail penetrate the silence, The three people sitting in the hallway came to their feet as one.

"It's here. The baby has come." John and Trace reached the door to Anne's room at the same time. But the doctor barred their way. His face told the story he could not put into words. "NO o o," John screamed. "Not my Annie." Trace swore under his breath while he and John tried to push the doctor aside.

"Maybelle is getting her all cleaned up. You can see her in a few minutes. Now why don't we all sit down." He turned to John, "I tried my best John. Tried everything I know but I just couldn't save her. We're lucky the baby is alive. By the way, it's a little girl. She's very fragile." He shook his head. "I don't know. We need a wet nurse right away."

Regina came out of the shock that had been holding her in it's grip. "One . . . one of my students just lost her baby two days ago. Her name is Alice Cox and she lives around the corner from the livery stable."

"In the meantime, fix some sugar in some warm water warm water and feed her a few drops. She will need milk as soon as possible."

Trace reached for his jacket. "It won't be long till daylight. I'll go see this woman."

The doctor tried to console John but he was inconsolable in his grief. He kept muttering, "Maureen, Mauren and now my Annie. Why is God punishing me?"

Regina pushed her own feelings aside and tried to comfort the grieving man. She could usually find the right words but this time they seemed shallow and unfeeling.

Trace came back in record time, "She's willing to help us and she'll be here in a few minutes."

"Now, I want to see Anne"

Maybelle had worked miracles. The haggard look was gone from Anne's r face and she looked serene and peaceful. Dressed in an ivory lace gown and robe, she looked like an angel. John had to be led from the room.

Maybelle had prepared a light supper but the mourners ate little. The discussion centered around the funeral. Due to the circumstances under which Anne and Trace had married, Trace did not object when John wanted Anne buried next to her mother rather than in the Burdette family plot.

*   *   *

The funeral service was over and the mourners' quickly left the cemetery. Trace, John and Regina stood looking down at the coffin resting in the rich earth. Nobody spoke until Maybelle said "I'se best be gittin back to the hotel in case some of them people come by ".

Only a few people came to the hotel and partook of the generous meal that had been provided by the church. Once the mourners left, Trace, John and Regina took up the subject of the baby. Alice was staying at the hotel for a few days until she could determine the baby's feeding pattern.

"What name have you chosen? Regina asked.

John looked at Trace and Trace turned to Regina.

"Oh, my goodness," Regina gasped. "Surely you don't want me to name her?"

"Well," John ventured, "we thought maybe she had talked about it with you."

"Yes, we did talk about it a couple of times. She did not want to name her after her mother. She said There was only one Maureen. It would have been painful for her."

"My mother's name was Lilly," John offered.

"My own mother was named Elizabeth Jean after her grandmother.", Trace added.

Regna was silent for a moment. "Why not name her Lillijean? All one word."

"LILLIJEAN?"

The men looked at one another and nodded "Lillijean it is," said Trace.

*     *     *

The days following Anne's death were a chaotic flurry of activity. Maybelle was retained to take over the household duties while Alice tended the baby. John was lost in grief and the only bright spot in his world was Lillijean. Trace seemed uncomfortable around the newborn, but Regina was enthralled. She had no experience with babies since she had no younger siblings. Anne had put together a layette that Regina added to with fancy items from the general store. After she finished her day at the school, she could be found with Lillijean in the room that had been Anne's.

"I wonder if she will have Anne's beautiful brown eyes?" Regina remarked one evening at supper.

John's swallowed hard and replied, "Yes, and Maureen had pretty brown eyes, too.".

Trace remained silent. He could see a hint of Alvin in Lillijean's features, but he could not say so in front of Regina. Finally, he spoke. "She's a pretty one all right."

Regina thought that Trace showed a reluctance to spend time with his daughter, but she did not mention it. After all, most men shied away from babies. It was when they learned to walk and talk that their interest perked up. Trace also seemed preoccupied and Regina thought it might be the thoughts that he had a motherless daughter to rear. But Trace was young and not unattractive. He would probably meet a young woman and marry her. For some reason Regina did not want to acknowledge, that thought seemed to dampen her spirits.

Marrying again was the furthest thing from Trace's mind. He was contemplating going to the sheriff and telling him about his job with the army, Grady, and the identity of the Klanners. Word had reached

Anderson about the Negro church that had been burned. Luckily no one had been injured. This should help Trace convince the sheriff to organize a posse. But first, he should meet with Grady. He wondered if the Klanners would include Grady in their next raid.

While Regina cleared the table, Trace spoke with John. "I'm going to ride tonight. Since that church was burned, we haven't heard anything so it's about time they made a move."

John glanced around to see that Regina was busy in the kitchen. "Please be careful. They won't hesitate to kill you if you run into them. Remember, you have a child to think about now."

Trace's jaw hardened. "I haven't forgotten my promise, John. I'm surprised you would think I would."

John's face colored. "I'm sorry Trace. It's just that . . . that." His voice choked up and he could not continue.

"I understand, John. Anne's loss has hit all of us hard."

*   *   *

Trace saddled Ulysess and headed for the abandoned smoke house. If Grady was not there, he would leave a note asking him to meet him in town at the saloon. They could then disappear separately and meet up to discuss their plans. Trace thought it was time to take the sheriff into their confidence. But he would not talk to the man until he spoke with Grady,

There was no sign of recent occupancy at the smoke house. Trace waited a few minutes until he could no longer risk being seen coming home at daylight. He scribbled a brief note and left it well concealed in one of the hiding places they had chosen.

That evening after supper and a little time spent with Lilijean, Trace ventured out to see if there was any sign of Grady. He did not recognize any of the horses tied in front of the Ace High Saloon. Grady could have changed horses. He decided to go inside. The room was not crowded as few men had money to buy liquor. He walled up to the bar and was greeted by W.A. Bay the owner of the Bay general store.

"Sorry about your loss, Burdette. Miss Anne was a fine woman."

"Yes, she was," Trace replied.

The barkeep stopped in front of Trace, a question on his lips.

`Make it beer,' Trace ordered.

Trace did not hurry but took his time drinking his beer. Nobody else approached him or offered to start a conversation. No use wasting any more time here. *I need to hit the more lively places.* He strode down the boardwalk, his boot heels trumping loud in the relative quiet of the night. After visiting two more saloons without a trace of Grady, Trace decided to call it a night. It was probably too soon for Grady to contact him.

As he left the last establishment, a man with a scruffy beard and the remnants of a Conferderate uniform, stopped him at the door. "Wherer you goin', bluebelly?"

Trace stiffened, his right hand bunched into a fist. "Home, where you ought to be if you got family."

The man's eyes squinted up and a grin showed tobacco stained teeth. "Don't reckon you'll have a home much longer. You and the *niggers* you're coddlin'."

"Are you threatening me?" Trace asked, his voice soft and quiet.

The man cackled, his fetid breath strong in Trace's face. "Nah, ain't me you got a worry about. But them night riders got you marked." He laughed again and turned away.

Trace was tempted to grab the man and question him. He looked around the saloon and there was not a friendly face among them. *Better to fight another day.* He tuned and left the room amid shouts and hoots of laughter.

# CHAPTER FOURTEEN

R EGINA PUT THE FINISHING TOUCHES on her toilette and surveyed herself in the mirror. The dark gray poplin skirt with its mini bustle fit smoothly over her hips and flowed gently to her ankles. A starched white blouse was lavishly trimmed in crotched lace around the collar and edges of the long sleeves. She knew the blouse would suffer from a day of teaching in the hot classroom. She had eliminated one of her three petticoats in difference to the heat, but by mid afternoon both she and the students were cranky and tired.

Before leaving for school, Regina peeked in to see Alice nursing the baby. What a thrilling sight that was, the white infant sucking hungrily at the black woman's breast. If she felt a touch of envy, Regina chalked it up to the fact that Anne had not had the opportunity to rear her child. How she wished she could provide sustenance for the infant. Maybe someday . . .

When she reached the school yard, Regina found two boys scuffling. She put a stern look on her face and marched up to them. "Stop it this instant!"

"Maam, it is his fault." The smaller of the two boys told her.

"It doesn't matter whose fault it is. You both will stand in the corner for ten minutes or until you can behave."

"But ma'am, he sed my momma's nursin' a white baby. That ain't true is it, ma'am?"

"Yes, it is true, but the baby's mother died and the baby has to have milk or it will die. Your mother lost her own baby and doesn't need the milk. It's a very generous thing she is doing and she's not to be talked about. Is that clear?"

The boys hung their heads and mumbled, "Yes um."

The rest of the day passed without incident and Regina dismissed the class early due to the extreme heat.

*   *   *

Trace made the rounds of the saloons but there was no sign of Grady. He didn't want to ride to the smoke house. He needed to cut his hours now that he had a daughter. She was in good hands but he still felt he should not be away from home too long.

He decided to go back to the hotel and tomorrow he would ride out to the farm. He needed to check on Moses and Jimbo. Moses had said he would send his grandson and get in touch with Trace if there was any trouble there. So far Trace had seen no sign of the young man. But he needed to check things out anyway.

When Trace reached the hotel, he spent a few minutes watching Lillijean who was sleeping contently beside Alice.

"She done took her early nighttime feedin'." Alice, said.

Trace looked at the sleeping infant and thought how proud Alvin would be of his daughter. Her pink rosebud mouth was turned up at the corners and he wondered if babies dream. What he knew bout babies would fit on the head of a pin. He grinned. *But I guess I'll learn.*

Trace smelled smoke when he opened the door to his room. Surely the hotel was not on fire! Just then a gravely voice broke the silence.

"Evenin' pard." Grady greeted him.

"Damn it, Grady, you scared the dickens out of me. How did you get in here anyway?"

The dim light from the hallway allowed Trace to light the lamp on the dresser. He closed the door. Grady was dressed in dark clothing. He had let his beard grow to a sizeable length. It would be easy to classify him as one of the Klanners.

"Sometimes it's easier to disappear right in the middle of a crowd than try to sneak around. But nobody saw me come in the hotel. I used the back door.'

"We need to contact the sheriff," Trace began the conversation.

"Are you sure he can be trusted?"

Trace shrugged. "I don't think we have much choice."

Later in the sheriff's office they heard the news that the General, his wife and both of his daughters had died in the epidemic.

"I'm sorry to hear that. The General was a good man. That might put a crimp in our plans," Trace responded.

"Naw, I don't think so. Maybe delay them a little though."

"You mind telling me what you're talking about?" the sheriff asked.

Trace and Grady exchanged glances. Trace started out by telling the sheriff about being recruited to scout for the Army and try to gather information on the Klanners.

Later Grady had come on the scene and they were working together. Grady had infiltrated the gang but was not taken on any of their raids.

"Guess they don't completely trust me," he grinned.

Trace identified the men he had recognized. He cleared up the mystery of the buckskin horse. "You know about the Negro church they burned about a week ago?"

"Yeah. Lucky thing nobody was hurt," Dawson said. "We need to get a posse together and corner them at that horse corral. 'Course we need to know when they will meet there." The sheriff looked at Grady.

"That's hard to say. They don't seem to have a regular pattern. The only thing I've noticed is they don't ride when the moon is full. Guess they figure they might be recognized. 'Sides the Negroes are superstitious and the dark of the moon helps the Klanners to do more dirty work."

"Do they ever meet there just to palaver?" the sheriff asked.

"Not very often," Grady answered.

"Well, we just got to find a way to know when and where they are going to strike."

"I'll do my best to find out and get word to you before hand. I can pretend I'm anxious to get in on the action. I got me an idea that might flush them out but it might take a while to set it up."

"Want to share your plan with us?" the sheriff inquired.

Grady grinned. "Not yet but I'll get word to you as soon as I can."

*     *     *

When Trace reached the hotel after bidding Grady goodnight, he saw the lamp was burning in the baby's room. He pushed the door all the way open and saw Regina sitting in the rocker with Lillijean in her arms. A lump rose in his throat when he thought of Anne and how she would have loved her child and nurtured it.

Regina looked up and smiled. "She had her early feeding, but she's a bit fussy. Alice went home to be with her family for a little while. I offered to look after Lillijean."

"You should be sleeping yourself. You have to face that roomful of younguns in the morning."

Regina nodded. "That's true but since that little fracas in the school yard, it has quieted down." She continued rocking the baby and soon the little one's eyes closed in sleep. She rose and placed Lillijean in her cradle and covered her with a light blanket.

Trace cleared away the lump in his throat. "Regina, I really appreciate your helping with the baby. I know you work hard at the school and it seems babies require a lot of time. I'm not sure how I'm going to work out a solution for her care but I will have to make better arrangements somehow."

Regina did not hesitate. "Trace, I love looking after Lillijean. She is such a sweet child, just like her mother. Besides, Anne was my very dear friend and the least I can do is help with her baby. If I weren't teaching, there would be no problem at all, but . . ."

"I think I understand but I don't want to take advantage of your generosity."

"If Lillijean wakes up I'll hear her. I don't know what I could do about it but maybe Alice will be back by then. Now try to get some sleep."

Regina bent and kissed the sleeping infant on the check. "Good night, Trace".

Trace could not sleep when he finally undressed and slipped under the covers. He thought of Lillijean and the long years ahead the child would be without a mother. He could remarry but he had married once without love and he was not going to do it a second time. An image of Regina with the baby in her arms slipped into his mind.

They made a pretty picture all right. She was pretty, educated and she loved Anne's child like it was her own. He shook his head. *Damn* Anne was hardly cold in her grave. He forced the thought away and drifted off to sleep.

Meanwhile, Regina was having similar thoughts. Stop it! Anne was her best friend and she was already coveting her husband? Noooo! It's just that Lillijean needed a mother. Besides, Trace was not interested in her. He was still grieving for Anne though he didn't show it. Trace would probably marry again but it would most likely be a farm girl who could take over the duties of a farm wife. What did she know about that? No, she must put that thought out of her mind.

Sleep did not come easy and Regina spent a restless night trying to keep her thoughts under control. When morning finally arrived, she vowed she would be a model of decorum and keep her distance from Trace.

*        *        *

Trace and John were sitting on the porch enjoying their after supper smoke. "Soon be the dark of the moon," Trace commented.

"Yeah," John replied. "Do you think they will ride soon?"

"Don't know but I wouldn't bet against it," Trace answered.

Regina appeared in the doorway rolling down the sleeves of her blouse. "The dishes are done and Maybelle has left for the night. The baby is nursing and, if you want to see her, she'll be sleeping soon."

Trace and John stood as Regina joined them on the porch. She seated herself in the rocker. "Please don't let me interrupt. It is much cooler here than in the lobby."

The men resumed their seats. Trace, still new at fatherhood replied, "I'll look in on Lillijean before I turn in."

Regina remained silent. She remembered her promise to act proper and lady like.

John faked a yawn and rose from his seat. "A batch of newspapers came in on the stage today and I haven't had time to look at them. I'll say goodnight now."

"Regina, I appreciate your help with the baby. You're not used to working so hard, I know. You probably had servants at home." Trace had noticed the tired look in her eyes and slump in her shoulders.

"Yes, we had a maid and a laundress besides the cleaning lady who came periodically to do the heavy cleaning. But, I don't mind helping out. And you know, I adore Lillijean."

"Yes, and I am grateful for that. A baby without a mother needs all the affection she can get."

"She's such a good baby. Hardly fusses except when she's hungry. Thank the Lord for Alice. I'm sorry her own child died but she's been a God send for Lillijean."

"Yes she has. I think I'll check with John on those newspapers. Will you be alright here on the porch?"

'Oh yes, but I think I will go inside. I have some papers to grade," Regina stood. "Good night, Trace."

"Good night." Trace dropped his cigarette, mashed it with his boot heel and threw the butt into the street. He followed Regina inside.

*   *   *

Trace rode to the old smokehouse late the next afternoon. There was a note from Grady that he would be there shortly after dark. Trace chewed on a piece of jerky he had in his saddlebags. He would like to have a cup of coffee but did not want to light a fire. He finished his repast with a drink of water from his canteen.

Ulysess snorted and stomped his feet. Trace faded into the darkness in the old building and waited. It was mostly likely Grady but you never could tell with renegades and good men alike roaming the countryside.

After several minutes, Grady appeared, grinning from ear to ear. "What's so funny". Trace asked, his voice harsh.

"Now don't get all huffy on me. I had to have a good excuse to get away tonight."

"And what excuse did you have?"

"Well, you know a man has his *needs* from time to time."

It was Trace's turn to grin. "Yeah, I know."

"I told them I had a little gal that was expecting me tonight."

"They believe that?"

"I think so," Grady replied. "Most of them are married men and they got a big laugh out of it."

"They would," Trace answered, his voice sour. The marriage between him and Anne had never been consummated and he had respected her too much to seek out female companionship.

Grady's expression turned serious. "They plan to ride next Saturday night. The moon will be dark and they have targeted a church just outside Brenham, that place called Watertown." He went on to give the details of when they would gather and what time they would strike.

"I guess they don't care that a small garrison is there. Just a chance to kill a few *bluebellies*. How many?" Trace asked.

"I'm not sure but probably around ten or fifteen. The rumor is that the Oliver boys may join in the fracas."

Trace grimaced. "That should put the icing on the cake. They are a tough bunch, to say the least. Well, it's up to the sheriff to pick his men. Anything else I should know?"

"That's all I know right now. If there is any change, I'll get in touch with you somehow."

"If I don't hear from you to the contrary, we will meet just outside Anderson in that abandoned factory. Right after dark."

Grady nodded. "I'm looking forward to this."

Trace's expression hardened. "So am I."

\* \* \*

Trace and John were enjoying a late evening smoke. Regina had retired for the night. "Lillijean is growing like a weed. Alice's milk surely agrees with her" John commented.

"Yes, I'd say it does."

"You know Trace, a baby needs more than milk to grow and thrive."

"Yes, I realize I'm not a very good father. I haven't been around children for many years, especially babies."

John chuckled. "You'll learn, son. You'll learn." Then John's tone turned serious. "Anne was twelve when her mother died. A big part of the raising was done. Not like Lillijean who will need somebody to teach her the things a mother would."

Trace thought of sweet gentle Anne who would have raised her daughter to be a lady. How was he going to bring up a child without a mother? Lillijean was Alvin's child and that might make the situation more difficult.

"Trace, I'm gonna be blunt. You ever thought of marrying again? Give Lillijeane the mother she needs. Lots of eligible women around who would make you a good wife."

Trace stared at John. *He was Anne's father! How could he think . . .* "God Lord, John. Anne has only been gone a month. How do you think I could have my mind on another woman?"

"I don't. But I also know yours was not a normal marriage. But you have to be practical. Regina is growing more and more fond of Lillijean and it will break her heart to have Lillijean taken away to the farm."

"I don't have any intention of taking the baby to the farm. She is much better off here with you and the women. I have this KKK business to worry about right now. Their plans to burn the church in Watertown have to be stopped and Grady and I plus the sheriff and his posse mean to stop them. There will be a fight, you know, and the outcome could be a disaster."

# CHAPTER FIFTEEN

THE RIDERS RODE SINGLE FILE as they followed the ridgeline to the valley below. A group of silent men in dark clothing on dark horses that melted into the blackness of the night. Each man occupied with his own thoughts, survival uppermost on their minds.

Sheriff Dawson rode at the head of the column followed by Trace then Grady. Shop keepers, the blacksmith, a saloon owner and several of Anderson's residents made up the posse. They reached the valley floor and the sheriff called a halt in low voice. Sounds carried long distances at night.

The men reined their horses in a tight circle and dismounted, stretching their cramped muscles. It had been a long ride to Brenham. Taking his canteen from the saddle horn, Trace took a long swallow of the tepid water. It might be awhile before he had another opportunity. He strode toward the sheriff who was scanning the darkness before them and listening intently.

"See or hear anything?"

The sheriff was silent for a moment. "No," he whispered. "You?"

"No, but I caught a whiff of smoke so something is burning," Trace answered.

Dawson sniffed noisily and nodded. "It's faint but up ahead. Let's ride."

The men mounted up and, mindful of the tangled brush on each side of the narrow trail, rode toward the thin cloud of smoke that appeared on the horizon. Trace judged they were a mile or so from Brenham and Watertown. Would they be too late to catch the Klanners?

The posse covered the distance in record time and when they burst out into the open, saw the large cross burning in the middle of the street. The

Klanners were milling about, yelling and shooting but no Negro people were outside their homes. The women and children were screaming and babies were crying and the Klanners whooped and hollered with joy.

Dawson gave the signal to charge into the melee and the posse drew their guns and started firing. The Klanners had failed to hear the posse approaching and were caught by surprise. Trace heard a bullet whistle by his ear. A dark form was bearing down on him and he fired. The man grabbed at his arm and yelled, "God damn nigger lovers."

Grady fired a volley of shots hitting one man in the thigh. The posse was not without wounds as one of the residents screamed when a bullet tore into his shoulder.

Smoke from the burning cross and the smell of gunpowder turned the street into a haze that made identifying the Klanners difficult. Unless a rider was within a few feet it was impossible to tell who wore hoods and who didn't. Somebody yelled, "Let's get out of here." The Klanners abandoned the fight and fled.

The people came out of their houses slowly, at first, then ran to the posse to thank them. They brought buckets of water to put out the fire and the stench was strong.

The sheriff talked with a man that seemed to be their spokesman. "Did you recognize any of the Klanners?"

"No suh, but they had bags over their heads."

"Well, I think the danger is over for now. We have a wounded man that needs tending. You got anybody that can take care of a bullet wound?"

"Yes, suh. Granny knows how to fix 'em."

The resident whose name was Steinhagen was taken to Granny's small house and his wound expertly cleaned and dressed. "Yo all might see the doctor when yo get back to Anderson'" she told him.

On the ride back to Anderson, Trace told the sheriff he was sure he hit one of the Klanners. "Best keep and eye out for somebody with a gunshot wound. He may show up at the Doc's himself. If you need me for anything, I'll be at the farm. I plan to ride out there later in the day."

The posse arrived back in Anderson as dawn broke. The sheriff thanked the men for their participation. "This might just be the first of these night rides providing we can get the word in time." The men were tired and hungry and quickly disbursed.

"I'll do my best to find out all I can." Grady promised.

"You be careful or they'll be on to you. I hate to think what would happen then," Trace cautioned.

"Yeah," Grady replied. "I sleep with one eye open and my gun where it's easy to reach."

Trace dismounted at the livery and Grady said he was going to hightail it back to the outlaw camp. If he took a short cut that he had found, he might arrive before the Klanners.

"I'll be in touch." He spurred his horse and was gone in a cloud of dust.

\*     \*     \*

It was nearly noon when Trace emerged from his room. He peeked into Lillijean's room and found her sleeping. He gazed at the rosebud mouth and ivory skin. Her little cap of wispy brown hair was lighter than Anne's, but he decided she looked more like Anne than Alvin.

"She be growing like a weed, Mr. Trace. Won't be no time till she recognize you and want you to hold her," Maggie told him.

"She sure is a pretty little thing," Trace was awkward around the infant and knew he didn't act very fatherly. John understood but he wondered if Regina thought it strange.

"Well. Good morning, Trace. I've been waiting for you to come down. What happened last night?"

Trace quickly filled John in. "Keep an eye open for a couple of wounded men. If they are from around here, they will probably show up at the doctor's. I'm going to clue him in before I leave town for the farm. I need to check on Moses and his grandson. He said he would send the boy to town if anything happened but I haven't seen any sign of him."

"No he hasn't been around the hotel so maybe everything is going alright I think the Klanners are more likely to go after the Negroes than anybody else."

"Yeah, you're probably right, but any white men who seem to favor the Negroes is at risk."

"Let Maybell fix you some breakfast before you leave. You need a good meal after all that activity last night."

"You're right about that. I think my ribs are sticking to my backbone."

After a hearty breakfast of eggs, bacon, biscuits and strong black coffee, Trace headed for the doctor's office.

125

The doctor had treated Steinhagen for his gunshot wound but no other men had appeared. "That Negro granny did a fine job. Now it just has to heal up although it's plenty sore. That should clear up in a few days."

"Keep your eyes open, Doc. And let me know if anyone turns up. I know one of them has a wounded thigh. Not sure but I think the other one got it in the shoulder."

*     *     *

Trace arrived at the farm with supplies and found Moses and Jimbo mucking out the barn. "Sorry I been so long getting out here but we had a little trouble with the Klanners." Trace gave an abbreviated version of the battle at Watertown.

"Maas Trace, you'uns better be real careful. Them Klanners is mean mens. Won't hesitate to shoot you or even hang you." Moses shuddered, remembering his dead grandson.

"I'm well aware of how vicious they can be, Moses. I just have to keep my guard up."

Trace spent the rest of the day putting away the supplies and tidying up the house. It has been neglected since Anne had gone to stay at the hotel. The sun went down and twilight spread over the land. "I think I'll spend the night here and go back to town in the morning. I could use a diversion." He informed Moses and Jimbo and told them he would cook supper since they had plenty of food on hand. The men beamed, thinking they would have a good meal even if Miss Anne was not there to cook it.

"How be your little baby, Massa Trace?" Moses inquired.

"Oh, she's fine, Moses. Growing like a weed. I'll bring her, Miss Regina and Alice out to visit one of these days."

"Alice be the wet nurse?"

"Yes, and a very good one, too."

Trace cooked some bacon, had brought biscuits from the hotel and made a pan of gravy. He opened tins of tomatoes and peaches which were a real treat considering the price and availability of like items.

"That be a mighty fine supper, Massa Trace," Moses complimented, using a bite of biscuit to sop up the last of the peach juice.

Trace knew he needed to do some thinking about a lot of things, but he also knew he had to keep his hands busy. He decided to sharpen some tools that would be needed when he could plant a crop again. Various thoughts ran through his mind: the task of raising Lillijean without a mother, and the violence being caused by the Klanners. Without warning, the thought of Regina popped into his head. Why was he thinking about her with Anne gone less than two months?

Trace knew Regina had loved Anne dearly and she loved Lillijean, too. But she was a city girl and not used to physical tasks that would be required of her if she lived at the farm. And if he did court her, would she think he was only looking for a mother for his child? She was pretty, educated and smart and he liked her well enough. No way am I going to marry again for convenience. He would just give it some time and see what developed. He could hear all the gossip that would arise should he court Regina openly and he would not do less.

*   *   *

The yellow fever epidemic continued to escalate. Henry Fanthrop succumbed to the disease in September. Dr. Parker was kept busy treating patients but there was little he could do. Those caring for the sick were exposed and several died of the fever. All social activities were suspended, but church services were held every Sunday. Somehow John and Regina escaped the fever and Regina continued to attend church.

As she was leaving the church one bright Sunday morning, a young man approached her. He doffed his hat and with a fashionable bow, introduced himself. "Miss Mills, my name is Joseph Hutcheson. I am an attorney and my office is just down the street from the hotel."

Regina was surprised at his bold actions but had long ago learned men on the frontier wasted little time with formalities. She smiled and answered, "I'm pleased to make your acquaintance, Mr. Hutcheson." She held out her hand which, instead of shaking it, he placed a light kiss on the back of her hand.

"May I accompany you to the hotel?"

Regina hesitated but his mile was so engaging she decided it would be proper. As they walked along, he offered small details about himself, his army service, his time spent at the university and after completing his education decided o travel west and begin a new life.

They reached the hotel and found John sitting on the porch. "Hello, John. And how are you this fine morning?"

John's eyebrows rose but he answered casually, "Hello, Joe. I'm fine."

Hutcheson turned to Regina, "Miss Mills I know you are not from here so that I cannot ask your father's permission to call on you, but I would be honored to do so."

"MY parents are dead, Mr. Hutcheson. I have been making my own decisions for some time now." Regina watched him closely for his reaction to her reply.

A twinkle appeared in his eye but his voice was serious when he told her, "Yes, I can see that since you came all the way to Texas to teach the Negro children."

A slight flush colored Regina's checks as she remembered David's objections to her decision. "My brother did object but, as I say, I make my own decisions. I wanted to do something worthwhile although I was a teacher in Indiana. Yes, Mr. Hutcheson, I would be pleased to have you call on me."

"You are most gracious, Miss Mills. Shall we say Wednesdays evening about seven o'clock?"

Regina nodded. "Yes, that would be fine."

Hutcheson smiled that same engaging smile. He took her hand again. "Thank you Miss Mills. I'm afraid the social life in town is nonexistent because of the fever, but I'm sure we can find things to talk about."

"Yes, I'm sure we can. I look forward to Wednesday evening. If you will excuse me, I must go and check on Lillijean." She didn't wait for his reply but turned and went into the hotel.

John and Joe discussed the situation in Anderson and other areas. "It is a terrible time for Texas," Joe replied.

"I agree with that. I just wonder how it is going to end?"

"I don't know, John, but we will be years getting back on our feet. Me included." Joe smiled ruefully.

"No doubt about it."

After several minutes of discussion, Hutcheson took his leave. Regina did not reappear and John knew she was totally occupied with Lillijean.

*   *   *

Trace came to town the next day. There wasn't much he could do on the farm, and he was anxious to hear from Grady. Word had spread about the confrontation at Watertown. and Trace was questioned by several men when he ventured into the saloon.

"Well well, look who's here, boys," Fred Collins spoke from a table where four men were playing a game of poker. "If'n it ain't the bluebelly."

Trace's eyes narrowed and he walked to the table. "Collins the war is over and it would be in your best interest to put it behind you."

"That so?" Collins rose from the table. "Maybe you need to be reminded of your Ma and Pa and how hard it was for them seein' as how they had a traitor for a son."

Trace felt his neck getting hot. The man wanted to fight but Trace wasn't having any of it. "Collins you always did have a big mouth. I'm not going to fight you. You're at least twenty years older than me and I was taught to respect my elders."

Collins face flamed a bright red. "I might be but I can still whip a coward like you."

It was Trace's turn to flush and his voice was harsh when he answered. "Think what you want. My decision to support the Union is none of your business Besides, I didn't see you wearing a Reb uniform."

Collins sputtered and finally managed to say, "I was turned down so I could furnish food and horses for the army."

Trace laughed but there was no mirth in his reply. "Yeah, if I remember correctly you started farming as soon as the call went out for volunteers."

"I . . . I," Collins was unable to speak Trace thought he was going to drop dead of apoplexy. "This discussion is over." He turned on his heel and left the saloon.

*     *     *

Regina received a letter from Nancy announcing that she and David were expecting an addition to their family. The news brightened Regina's day. The school was closed due to the epidemic and time was heavy on her hands. She spent as much time with Lillijean as possible, but the baby slept a lot. She began to help Maybelle with some of the chores and found she liked dusting and waxing the heavy furniture in the bedrooms. She added a touch of color here and there by using dried flowers and small pictures she bought at the general store.

She answered Nancy's letter with enthusiastic comments about the baby and advised her to take good care of herself. She did not mention the results of Ann's pregnancy for fear of frightening Nancy and David. She wondered if she would be back in Indiana in time for the birth. The future of teaching did not look very bright at the moment. The mail was often nonexistent due to the epidemic and she wondered how long it would take for her letter to reach them.

Regina wandered into the kitchen one afternoon where Maybelle was preparing the evening meal. "What are we having, Maybelle?" she inquired.

"You know how them men folks like they's fried chicken. Well, the store just got a few chickens in from some farmer whose leaving town and wanted to get rid of them. I took one, a nice young pullet."

"That sounds delicious. I like the way you fix it."

`Miss Regina, I know you is a lady and all, but since there ain't no school, would you like to learn a little about cookin'?"

Regina smiled and her face lighted up. She had never been allowed to help Hannah with any of the household chores, but she always had a secret desire to learn how to make the wonderful desserts they had on special occasions. "Thank you Maybelle. I'm sure I will be more hindrance than help, but I would like to learn."

The afternoon passed swiftly and Regina first cooking lesson was a success. Maybe started her on the simple task such as washing the greens which were to accompany the meal. Regina realized there was not the wealth of staples and ingredients she was accustomed to but the substitutions proved just as tasty.

That night at supper Maybelle proudly announced that Regina had helped prepare the meal. Trace stared at Regina and she smiled. There was a lot more to learn but with a good teacher like Maybelle she could master the art of cooking.

Trace was astounded that Regina had enjoyed the time she spent in the kitchen. It had lifted her spirits until her eyes shined and her face was glowing. *Well who would have thought a pampered city girl would want to learn how to cook. But, then, she's made of stern stuff.*

"Congratulations, Regina, you've done yourself proud.," John complimented her.

"Oh, no, I just followed Maybelle's directions but she did most of the work."

"She did well, Massa John. All she needs is a little more practice. That be, if'n she wants to do it again."

"Yes, yes, Maybelle, I do want to learn more. I really enjoyed what we did today and I know there is a lot more to learn. May I join you tomorrow afternoon about the same time?"

"Yes'um. I be pleased to have you. You learn quick and it won't be no time till you be a real good cook."

Regina beamed and Trace couldn't help but chuckle inwardly. The city girl was becoming a woman of the frontier.

# CHAPTER SIXTEEN

JOSEPH HUTCHESON CALLED ON REGINA and they sat talking in the room off the lobby. Anne had made it into a small parlor with comfortable chairs A round table in the center of the room held an ornate oil lamp.

"Tell me about yourself, Miss Mills," Hutcheson opened the conversation.

"There really isn't much to tell, Mr. Hutcheson. As you know, I came from Indiana to teach in Texas. I saw it as an opportunity to do something important. Not that my teaching in Indianapolis was not important," she hastened to add.

"Oh, I'm sure it was. Tell me about it."

"I taught at a Christian elementary school. My brother is the vice principal there."

Regina thought of David and Nancy and the child they were going to have. A wave of homesickness washed over her. If the situation did not change in Anderson, she might well be going back to Indiana in the spring.

Hutcheson watched Regina carefully and correctly surmised she missed her home in the North. What could he do to encourage her to stay in Texas? He wanted to marry and raise a family and Regina was an excellent candidate—pretty, educated, and a lady. She would make a fine wife for an attorney

"Do you miss the cultural events the city had to offer?" he questioned.

Regina nodded her head. "Yes, I do. Especially the music and the theater. We have a fine opera house in Indianapolis. The theater companies come from all over to perform there. It's an elegant building with a large theater and a spacious ballroom."

"I understand. I miss that too. When I was at the university in Virginia, I attended many fine productions."

Hutcheson could see that Regina's mind was elsewhere and shortly took his leave. He would call on her again if she permitted it. She was definitely a candidate for marriage. The fact that she was pretty didn't hurt matters any. "May I call again, Miss Mills?"

"You may, sir." Indeed Regina's mind was on Lillijean. She wanted to tuck the baby in for the night. As soon as she had bid Hutcheson goodnight, she hurried to the child's room. The infant was awake, her pretty features relaxed. Asking Alice's permission, she picked up the baby and settled in the rocking chair. She hummed Braham's lullaby as she rocked and Lillijean was soon sleeping soundly.

*   *   *

Trace stabled his horse and walked toward the hotel. He had not made contact with Grady, and he was afraid that the scout had met with bad luck. He would just have to wait and see if Grady showed up. Trace reached the hotel and found John sitting on the porch.

"Trace are you interested in Regina?" John came straight to the point. His granddaughter needed a mother.

Trace felt his face growing hot. "Good Lord, John, where did that come from?"

"If you are you'd best be letting the lady know. Joe Hutcheson has come calling."

"Joe Hutcheson? How did that come about? I didn't know he even knew Regina."

"They go to the same church and he walked her home last Sunday. Regina gave him permission to call on her. After all, she's not getting any younger and Joe would be a good catch."

"Much better than a poor farmer and traitor to The Cause." Trace's voice reflected the bitterness that had not left him.

"You have a fine farm, Trace, and once this mess is cleaned up, you will be able to plant your crops."

'The state government and the federal government don't see eye to eye on anything. Can't much get done until they do. If they ever do."

Trace heard her light footsteps before she appeared in the doorway. Regina's face was flushed and she looked happier than he had seen her since Anne's death. Hutcheson was right behind her.

133

The men exchanged greetings and Hutcheson stated he must be going. "I'll see you on Sunday Miss Mills. You promised I could walk you home from church. I hope you don't change your mind.:

"I always keep my promises, Mr. Hutcheson," Regina assured him.

*Damn!* Did he want to get involved in a love triangle. Trace wasn't ready to marry again but it would be the practical thing to do. And, he had to admit, it bothered him that Hutcheson was courting Regina. What should he do about it? He thought Regina would be flabbergasted if he declared himself.

"Good evening. Trace. I'm sorry you missed supper. Can I fix you anything?" Regina asked.

"No ma'am. I had supper at the farm. But thank you for offering." Trace was having difficulty keeping his voice natural. Thoughts of Regina and Joe Hutcheson kept running through his mind.

"I'll say goodnight, then. I want to look in on Lillijean."

"I'll go with you. I need to see my little girl." Trace followed Regina up the stairs.

The baby was in her cradle fast asleep. She looks like an angel, Trace thought. Her little rosebud mouth was closed in a tiny smile. Oh, God, how much she looks like Anne. Anne would be pleased if he married Regina, but I just can't do it. Not right now, anyway. Besides, she is interested in Joe or she would not let him court her.

"Oh, Trace, she is so beautiful!" Regina touched the Lillijean's soft cheek and placed a light kiss on her forehead.

"Yes she is." Trace answered and before he realized it his arm had gone around Regina's shoulder. He heard her light gasp and immediately withdrew his arm. "I'm sorry, Regina, I didn't mean to . . ."

Regina did not move. "It's all right, Trace. After all, we are good friends."

"Yes, yes, we are." His voice was hoarse. "And, I really appreciate what you do for Lillijean. I know Anne would be happy about it." He just could not bring himself to say more. Maybe in time, but he might not have much time with Joe in the picture.

Grady appeared late that night. Trace grabbed for his revolver which was on the night table beside his bed. Grady's arm shot out and caught his hand.

"Easy does it pard."

"Grady! I could have killed you!"

Grady laughed. "I don't think so. I've got too many years on you doing this kind of work." Trace sat up and reached for his clothes he had discarded on the chair near his bed. He dressed quickly and faced Grady who had taken a seat in the rocking chair. "What's the latest on the Klanners?"

"Well. Pard, I think they might be onto me. So I packed up my gear when I left."

"I'm surprised they let you leave." Trace's blood ran cold thinking what they could have done to Grady.

"They didn't. I waited till they were all asleep. They had been pulling on a jug of moonshine and were snoring away."

"You were lucky."

"Yeah," Grady agreed. "In more ways than one. Bickerstoff rode in with several of his men yesterday. They are planning to hit Anderson and burn the school and the churches especially that little building where the Negro people go to church."

"Bickerstoff? They are really bringing out the big guns. He's a killer for sure." Trace had heard of the man's reputation and it was as black as the people he had killed.

"Yeah. The sheriff needs to raise a lot more men than we had last time."

"That might be a hard thing to do. A lot of the town folks have left due to the fever. But if the Klanners show up, the others will come out and defend their property."

"We need to see Dawson as soon as it gets light." Trace buckled on his gunbelt and slipped his revolver in the holster. He had taken to wearing a weapon now that the raids could come any time. There had been a few instances when the Klanners struck during the day.

"Did they mention when they were going to strike?"

"Not exactly. But probably in the next day or so. Mind if I stretch out on your bed for awhile seeings as how you are up and dressed."

"No, go ahead. You're probably tuckered out from that quick getaway." Trace grinned. "I'm going to the kitchen and make a pot of coffee. Want me to call you when it's done?"

"Yeah, providing you let me sleep for an hour or two." Grady had slipped off his boots and gunbelt and lay back on the bed fully clothed.

Trace tiptoed out of the room and down the stairs. He did not want to wake anyone this time of night. It was dark but it wouldn't be long till dawn. The sheriff usually arrived at his office after a late breakfast. He patrolled the streets after the saloons had closed and did not make it to bed until after midnight.

Trace was not familiar with the hotel kitchen and looking for the coffee knocked a tin off the shelf above the stove. It hit the floor with a clatter. *Damn it! Clumsy oaf!* He heard the footsteps on the stairs and decided he better light a lamp before somebody got hurt.

"Who's there?" John called out.

"It's me. Trace. I'm sorry I woke you. I was looking for the coffee."

"What are you doing up at this time of night? Or should I say morning since it will soon be dawn."

"Grady finally showed up. Seems the Klanners are going to strike Anderson soon."

John's face blanched. "Good God, the town is all but deserted. What are we going to do?"

"We're going to inform the sheriff as soon as Grady wakes up. He rode hard to get here and was nearly tuckered out." Trace found the coffee tin and began to grind the beans.

A banked fire had been left in the big range and John poked it to life. He filled the pot with water and Trace dumped the coffee in it. "It will take awhile for the water to boil."

"We need to warn the townspeople but I don't want to start a panic. I think I will let the sheriff decide how he wants to do that." Trace was not eager to take on the job.

"Dawson is a good man and experienced in handling rough situations but this could mean a lot of bloodshed."

"No doubt about it. Just be careful and keep an eye on this place. We don't want any fires close to the hotel." Trace was thinking of his infant daughter and Regina. They were upstairs and might not be able to get out if the building caught fire. Thank the Lord it was made of brick.

The aroma of brewing coffee filled the room. "I don't think I'll wake Grady just yet. He needs to sleep a little longer."

"I can start breakfast if you want to eat," John volunteered.

"I think I'll wait for Grady. But I will have a cup of that coffee when it's ready."

The coffee was scalding hot and Trace refrained from taking a sip. "Is Maybelle coming in today?"

"Yes, I think she is going to give Regina some more cooking lessons." John grinned. "Sure never thought I'd see that young lady working in the kitchen."

"Neither did I but you can never tell about people."

"Regina is a lady, no doubt, but when she sees a need or feels she needs to help out, she don't hesitate." It was plain John had the highest regard for the young woman.

"That coffee sure smells good," Grady spoke from the doorway.

John reached for another cup and filled it with the steaming brew. "Be careful. It's hot as Hades."

The dawn had faded away and light filtered into the room. The three men moved to the table with their coffee.

"I think we need to begin making a few preparations," Grady told them.

# CHAPTER SEVENTEEN

WITH THE ADVANCE WARNING GRADY gave them, Sheriff Dawson was able to recruit several men from the town and surrounding farms. He placed the men at the most strategic places. It was after midnight when the riders appeared on the darkened street. Trace counted twelve of them and the buckskin horse was in the lead. They began to light their torches and shots rang out. The men were ready and the Klanners hesitated, surprised at the volley of gunshots coming from the shadows. "It's an ambush! Git them torches lit," the leader yelled and proceeded to return the gunfire.

The school house was nearer than the church and they turned their horses in that direction. Just as they reached the building, the man carrying a lighted torch tumbled from his horse. Another rider swooped down and picked up the torch, but he too was hit. He threw the torch into the grass and immediately it caught fire. He spurred his horse into the nearby brush. The fire quickly spread to the building and the flames ignited the old dry wood. There was no way to save the structure and it was not near other buildings. It would be best to let it burn.

Trace left his hiding place near the hotel and sprinted toward the cover of the mercantile. A bullet whizzed by and he felt it burn the skin on his arm. That was close!

He did not know where Grady was but hoped the scout was all right. The street was filled with dust, and torches which had been abandoned. The Klanners seem to gather their wits and formed a beeline for the church. Some of the townspeople left their posts and gunfire erupted in a loud volley. And between the dust and the smoke from the torches and the burning school house, it was hard to identify anyone.

Grady was already at the church and opened fire when the Klanners were in range. As he stepped back for cover, a bullet found its way to him and lodged in his arm. He bit back the pain and reached for his neckerchief to staunch the flow of blood he knew was coming. At least it's not my gun hand. He continued firing and the Klanners drew back a few feet. Another one of them screamed, "I'm hit, I'm hit" and kicked his horse into a run in the opposite direction.

The Klanners decided they had had enough. "Let's get out of here," the leader yelled. They quickly turned tail and headed out of town. There was no point in chasing them. The townspeople came out into the street to survey the damage. The Klanners objective was to burn the school house and church but they had been out foxed and the church remained intact.

After the Klanners rode away, the townspeople began to see to the burning school house. They carried buckets of water to wet the ground thereby insuring the fire would not spread. After several minutes the roof collapsed and the building was a smoldering pile of rubble.

"I think this calls for a drink," said the saloon keeper. "Drinks on the house." Several of the men, covered in dirt and ashes followed him to his establishment.

Trace found Grady and saw he was wounded. "Better get you over to Doc's. The drinks can wait."

Grady, pale beneath his tan, nodded. "It does hurt some."

The sheriff found where the two Klanners had been hit but the bodies were gone. The Klanners had managed to pick up their wounded or dead companions. "We'll get better sign in the morning."

"You don't aim to try to find 'em?" one of the men asked.

"No, but we might find something that would tell us who they might be. Let's take advantage of that free drink. I think we've earned it.'

The doctor took one look at Grady's arm and said, "That bullet has to come out."

"Yeah, this ain't the first time I been winged." Grady responded. "Get at it."

Trace marveled at the way Grady kept his composure when the doctor dug the bullet out of his arm. He was one tough nut. But you could tell it hurts like hell. Good thing it was not his gun hand.

The doctor finished bandaging the wound. "You need to favor that arm for a few days. I had to go pretty deep and you've lost a lot of blood. Come back tomorrow afternoon and let me take a look at it."

Grady nodded and laid a wad of bills on the table. "Thanks, Doc."

Back at the hotel, Trace suggested Grady go to his room and lie down.

"He can have the room next to yours, Trace. I think he will be comfortable there."

"Much obliged John. I think I will turn in." As he started up the stairs, Regina came hurrying out of the baby's room. He stepped aside to let her pass.

"Trace, are you all right?" Regina's voice revealed her concern.

"Yeah, I'm fine. Grady caught one in the arm." Trace acknowledged.

"Oh, I'm sorry, Mr. Hawkins. I didn't mean to ignore you. Is there anything I can do?"

Grady grinned, So that's the way the wind blows. "No ma'am. I just need to catch me a little shut eye. I'll see you folks in the morning." He made short work of shucking his clothes and crawling into bed. *I am a might tuckered out.* The laudumn the doctor had insisted he take had dulled the pain. In a matter of minutes he was asleep.

Trace and John discussed the shoot out. "Do you think they will come back?" John asked.

"I doubt it. The reception they got was more than they bargained for," Trace replied. "I'm awful sorry about the school house, Regina."

"Even though it was closed, I was looking forward to the reopening. I don't know what will happen now. I hate to think there will be no schooling available when the epidemic is over."

"The Bureau will find another building." John tried to assure her. If they did not, then Regina would return to her family and he didn't want that to happen.

"You're too good a teacher for the Bureau to let you go." Trace would hate to see her leave. And, it had little to do with Lillijean although he tried to convince himself that was the reason.

"I will just have to wait until I hear from Mr. Shields.".

\*    \*    \*

It was a beautiful October day. The weather was cooler and some of the leaves were beginning to turn. After the first frost came, they would burst into full color. The epidemic seemed to be running its course although there were still cases being reported.

Trace was on his way to the farm to check on Moses and Rufus. He had supplies tied behind his saddle and the rumble in his stomach told him it was nearing the noon hour. Moses and Rufus were probably low on vittles. He would cook something when he reached the farm.

Moses and Rufus came out to meet Trace as he rode up to the house.

"Mssa Trace, we's been lookin' fur you." Moses was grinning from ear to ear.

Trace dismounted and shook the old man's hand. "I would have been here sooner, but the Klanners struck Anderson a couple of nights ago. Luckily we had been warned so they were foiled in their attempt to burn everything." They did manage to burn the school house but not the church."

Moses eyes grew wide as did Jimbo's. "Oh my Massa Trace. Was anyones hurt?"

"Only a couple of flesh wounds. Let me get these supplies and I'll cook us up something to eat."

Jimbo stepped forward. "I'se will do that, Mssa Trace."

After a meal of bacon, fried potatoes and biscuits brought from town, the men went out onto the porch. Tobacco was passed around and Trace and Jimbo built cigarettes while Moses filled a battered old pipe. There was no conversation for several minutes when Trace spoke. "I have never asked you about Alvin, Moses. Were you here the day he died?"

Moses hesitated. Taking the pipe out of his mouth, he, spat on the ground. "Masa Trace, I never told nobody but I was in my camp when I heard men and horses. Massa Alvin was a plowin' and he didn't have no weapon. Them riders had sacks over they heads and they wanted Massa Alvin to join 'em. He didn't want no part of that bunch"

"How many were there?"

"I don't rightly know, maybe five or six."

"Was one of them riding a buckskin horse?" Trace had his suspicions about Fred Collins when he first arrived in town.

Moses features showed his surprise. "Yes, Massa Trace. One of them horses was a buckskin."

Trace felt his anger rise but he held it back. "What happened when Alvin refused to join up with them?"

"Well . . . they's spooked the old horse and it pulled Massa Alvin along until the plow hit a big rock and Massa Alvin fell and hit his head on that rock. Then they's looked him over. They said he was daid. I didn't stay around after that. I hightailed back to my camp. They's didn't know about me and I kept still when the sheriff come nosin' around the next day."

Trace choked back the gall that arose in his throat. The Klanners had killed his brother the same as if they had pulled the trigger and shot him. But how could he prove it without betraying Moses trust? There had to be a way. There were some things he could do in the house and he needed time to think. He spent the rest of the afternoon tidying up and putting things in order but a way to confront Fred Collins eluded him.

The next morning Trace and Grady were summoned to the sheriff's office.

"How's that arm?" Dawson asked Grady.

"Sore as hell," Grady replied, "But it's healing."

"Sheriff, did you find any sign from that fracas with the Klanners?"

"Naw, nothing but a lot of spent shells and some blood on the ground."

Trace shook his head. "They are as slippery as eels, that's for sure."

"Grady, you up to riding?" Dawson asked.

"Depends," Grady answered.

"I've been thinking about them Klanners and that place where they keep their horses. Might be a good idea to pay them a visit. If they ain't at home we can run off their horses. That would cause them a little inconvenience."

"But if they are at home, we could have one hell of a fight on our hands." Trace spoke up.

Dawson grinned but his eyes were cold when he answered. "True, but at least we would have the chance to eliminate some of the dirty bastards."

"Or get eliminated ourselves." Trace returned.

"That's a chance we take. Every day when I pin on this badge and holster my gun before I leave the house, I take a chance that I won't be coming back."

"I can lead you to their camp." Grady agreed, "but if we go in the daytime, I doubt they will be around."

"Let me think on it awhile. I can't raise much of a posse but I'll talk to some of the men. I'll be in touch.'

*　　*　　*

Regina was in the parlor with Joe Hutcheson when Trace returned from his nightly walk around the town. He liked to check things out, especially the saloons where talk was loose. A few drinks always greased the patrons' tongues and he could pick up useful information.

"Hutcheson is becoming a regular visitor," Trace grunted.

"Yes he is and if you don't do something about it, you're going to lose your chance. She would make you a good wife, Trace and a good mother for Lillijean," John warned.

"Hell, John, what would a woman like her want with a man like me? She's educated, comes from a well to do family, everything I'm not."

"I don't think that means a hill of beans to Regina. And it's not just because of Lillijean. She is fond of you, I can tell. But you'll never know if you don't talk to her."

Trace did not reply and John dropped the subject.

Regina and Hutcheson came out of the parlor just as Trace started up the stairs. They exchanged pleasantries and Trace continued on to Lillijean's room. Alice had just finished feeding her and when she saw Trace, her face broke into a big smile.

"Massa Trace, she be wide awake. Would you like to hold her till she goes to sleep?"

Trace hesitated then let Alice place the baby in his arms. She was warm and smelled of milk and baby powder. He took a seat in the rocker and Alice gathered up her shawl.

"I'se be goin' home now but I be back to give her mornin' feeding. She sleep almost all night now and don't need a midnight feedin'."

"Thank you, Alice. We're very grateful to you."

"I be glad I can help out. She a sweet baby and don't hardly fuss at all. Good night, Massa Trace."

"Is your husband waiting for you>" Trace asked. "If he isn't, I'll walk you home. You shouldn't be alone on the street."

"Yes, Henry be waiting' downstairs."

\*     \*     \*

Sheriff Dawson showed up at the hotel the next morning. "I've gathered a few men together. I want to ride out to the horse corral. Trace, you and Grady will have to show us the way."

143

"You realize, sheriff, that we could end up in a gun fight," Grady cautioned.

"I'm fully aware of that and I explained it to the men Your arm healed enough to go?"

"Yeah. Besides it wasn't my gun hand that was shot." Grady had taken off the sling the doctor put on.

Trace had remained silent during the exchange. "It might be better to wait till dark to ride up on them.".

"No, that would be too risky. If we have daylight in our favor we can tell whether they are in the camp or not.'

"When you plan on leaving, sheriff? Grady asked.

'Daylight tomorrow. That all right with you?

"Trace nodded "Good a time as any, I guess.' We'll be ready and meet you at the livery stable."

Daylight came too soon and the men gathered at the livery stable. There was some muttering, but for the most part they were silent. Each man knew he might not be coming back and that put a pall over them.

The sheriff took the lead with Trace and Grady behind him. When they came to the place where they had to ride single file, the posse halted. "Hawkins, you take the lead since you're more familiar with the area."

They made frequent stops to listen and survey their surroundings. The brush began to thin out and around the bend they saw a large clearing. The posse halted and the men drew their guns. But there was no sign of the Klanners. The horses in the corral nickered and greeted the riders as they came closer.

"Some fine looking horseflesh," the sheriff commented.

Trace was looking for the buckskin and found it in the middle of the herd. He hesitated then said "See that buckskin over there?"

All eyes turned to the frisky horse. He was a fine looking animal with wide intelligent eyes and a smoky black mane and tail. "That's the horse one of them rode when they destroyed my cotton field and he showed up in town the night of the fire. He belongs to Fred Collins."

"You sure about that?" Dawson asked.

"Yes, I'm sure." Trace would tell the sheriff what Moses had revealed to him, but not in front of the posse.

Some sixth sense must have told the sheriff not to question Trace. "Come on boys, let's give them hay burners a little taste of freedom."

. The posse uncoiled their lariats while Grady opened the corral gate and rode inside. With a rebel yell, he swung his rope at the excited horses and they began to mill around, bolted for the open gateway, raising an enormous cloud of dust. The riders were, yelling and swinging their lariats, urged them on.

The animals hesitated outside the gate, then sensing freedom began to scatter in all directions. Trace thought about roping the buckskin but decided against it. He would have to explain to the others and the time was not right.

\* \* \*

Tired, dirty and hungry, Trace returned to the hotel in late afternoon. Contrary to his army training, he had not shaved and knew he must look like the desperados that roamed the country side. Regina was rocking the baby when he started for his room. Hoping she wouldn't see him, he tip toed along the hall.

But Regina's hearing was acute. She stood up, Lillijean in her arms and came to the doorway. "Trace! You're back. Are you all right? I was so worried."

'Yeah. The Klanners were not at the horse corral. We turned their horses loose so we can expect some kind of retaliation."

"Oh, dear. What do you think they will do?" Regina held Lilijean tighter and the baby emitted a soft cry. She soothed the child but her concern was written all over her face.

Maybe John was right and he should speak to her. See how she felt about Hutcheson. But he voiced none of these thoughts. "I need to scrub this dirt off. John said he would bring up some hot water."

"I'll bet your hungry, too. As soon as Alice comes to tend the baby, I'll fix you some breakfast."

A grin appeared on Trace's stubbled face. "Yeah, we didn't take any rations with us other than some jerky and that don't fill a man up."

John appeared with a bucket of hot water. "This should help some. If you need more, let me know."

Alice arrived and Regina relinquished the baby for her morning feeding. Lillijean was growing plump and healthy. Alice said she was beginning to recognize people and would smile and coo whenever Regina held her.

Trace came out of his room. He had shaved, bathed and changed his clothes. Regina thought he looked handsome and fit in spite of the dark circles under his eyes. "I'll make you some breakfast now."

"Thank you." Trace stepped back to let Regina go down the stairs. He watched as her skirts swayed around her ankles. *Nice looking backside.* Trace chastised himself for the thoughts that ran through his mind.

"John has made coffee if you would like some now," Regina told him.

"Yeah, I need something to keep me awake."

"Oh, you need some sleep."

"Yeah, but I have to meet with the sheriff this morning."

After a hearty breakfast of eggs, bacon and biscuits, Trace felt a lot better. Regina's culinary skills had benefited from Maybelle's teaching. She was still learning but had gotten past the basics and was into pastries and other desserts. It surprised her as much as it did the others that she enjoyed cooking. She couldn't help being a little proud of her accomplishments. Nancy was amazed when Regina wrote to her about the lessons and how much she had learned. Nancy was having a difficult pregnancy and Regina wished she could be with her at this time. But she was not ready to leave Texas.

# CHAPTER EIGHTEEN

T HE SIGNS OF AUTUMN WERE evident; warm days and cool nights. The smell of food being preserved, canned and dried permeated the air. The bounty of the kitchen gardens had been harvested, and only the vivid orange pumpkins and butternut squash remained. Nestled among the green vines, they presented a serene picture that belied the violence that enveloped the land.

Regina stood before the mirror and surveyed her reflection. Joe Hutcheson was coming to call and she wanted to look her best. The blue poplin dress with its ruffled neckline and hem complemented her fair skin and brown eyes. Regina knew that Joe was getting serious and she dreaded a proposal she knew was coming. She liked Joe and respected him but she admitted to herself that she did not love him. Maybe she had better think about it. She wasn't getting any younger and may not get another chance to marry. She wanted a home and a family.

Regina met Trace on the stairway as he left for his nightly patrol. "You look mighty fetching tonight, Regina. Is Joe coming to call?" He felt a pang of something akin to jealousy but his voice did not betray his feelings.

"Good evening, Trace," Regina replied, her cheeks colored a faint pink. "Yes, Joe is calling on me this evening."

"Sounds like things are getting serious."

Regina's cheeks grew bright pink. "Joe has said nothing to indicate his feelings are more than friendship."

"Yeah," Trace answered, his tone skeptical.

"You look lovely tonight, Regina." Joe Hutchinson told her as she met him in the hotel lobby.

They had been on a first name basis for several weeks.

"Thank you," Regina replied. Joe was a most considerate man. Always attentive and polite.

"Would you care to take a walk? It's quite pleasant this evening."

"Yes, that would be lovely. I'll get my shawl."

Regina turned toward the stairs and saw that Trace was leaning on the desk where John was working. He had a strange look on his face as he looked from Regina to Joe.

Trace had already had a short conversation with Joe about the epidemic and he learned that Mrs. Fanthrop had succumbed that day. Her death left only the Fanthrop's daughter and son-in-law to take over the inn. Trace wondered if they would keep it open or sell the property.

"I wish there was more entertainment in Anderson," Joe said as he and Regina walked along the boardwalk. There were few people on the streets but the saloons were busy as usual.

"It would be nice to see a stage production,"

Regina responded.

"San Antonio has a fine opera house," Joe old her. "Maybe not as fine as the ones in Indiana, but it is quiet elegant."

"I would like to go to San Antonio sometime. I hear it is a lovely place with some fine homes and shops." Regina's voice held a wistful note.

"Perhaps we could go there sometime," Joe's face colored slightly.

Regina's eye grew wide in surprise. Surely Joe knew she would not accompany him to San Antonio without a proper chaperone.

*I'm getting the cart before the horse.* Joe chastised himself. He'd better make his intentions known before Regina sent him packing. "Are you ready to go back to the hotel? If you are, I would like to talk to you about the future."

Shock replaced the testy reply she had planned to make. Was this it? Was Joe going to purpose?. She sincerely hoped not. She thought about Trace and her feelings for him which she had not admitted to herself. Trace had never given her the slightest hint that they were more than friends.

"Yes, I think it's time to go back to the hotel. It will be full dark in a short while."

The couple did not speak on the way back to the hotel. When they reached the lobby Regina saw the parlor was empty. "Would you like to go into the parlor?"

"Yes, that would be nice," Joe said removing his hat. He took the shawl from Regina's shoulders and placed it on the back of a chair.

Joe swallowed hard. This was going to be more difficult than he thought. Regina did not immediately sit down and Joe stood and took her hands in his. Might as well get started.

"Regina, we've been seeing one another for a couple of months. I enjoy your company and hopefully you enjoy mine.' As she started to speak, Joe shook his head." No, let me finish We have a lot of common interests and both of us are old enough to make good decisions. I am very fond of you, Regina and I would like you to be my wife."

Regina gasped. She thought Joe might propose but not this soon. "Joe, I don't know what to say. Two months is not very log to get to know someone. Yes, I enjoy your company and I'm glad you enjoy mine. I like you very much but that's not enough for marriage."

Joe's face, mirrored his disappointment and Regina quickly added, "I think we both need more time to get acquainted."

""Then you're not turning me down?"

"Oh no," Regina hastened to add. "It's just that I think it's too soon to talk of marriage."

"Then I can continue to call on you?"

"Of course," Regina smiled at the relieved look on Joe's face.

""Maybe Sunday after church we could go for a ride in the country."

"Yes. I'd like that."

*   *   *

Grady showed up a few days later. He had been to the army garrison in Brenham and made a full report on the Klanners attack on Anderson. He brought the pay that was owed to Trace.

"Our orders are to keep after them just like we been doing. But we need to step up our investigation and expose some of them."

"I know Fred Collins is in this up to his eyeballs. And I think he killed my brother, too."

"You got any proof about your brother?"

"Yeah, but it's a touchy situation. The man who saw it happen is afraid to testify and I'm not sure they would let him anyway."

"It's going to be harder to track them down. They won't be using that old hideout anymore." Grady's expression was thoughtful. "The only way we could catch them is to lay some kind of trap."

"Yes and I think I know a way to do it. You remember before the war we used to have them camp meetings?" Trace grinned remembering how he and Alvin had gotten into mischief at more than one of those meetings. "After the preacher finished and it got dark we would build a big fire and the fiddlers would play them old religious songs. What if we could arrange one of them meetings and be sure the Klanners heard about it?"

Grady nodded. "I know it's risky but if we planned it careful enough, we might be able to catch some of them."

"It's worth a try." Trace agreed. "You better make yourself scarce until we get this thing nailed down. We should have it when the moon is dark which will be a week or so.

"I'll get some of the Negroes together but think I will start by feeling Maybelle and Alice out. We could even say we are trying to raise money for a new school house."

"In the meantime, I'll lay low and keep my eyes open. You going to talk to Dawson?"

Trace nodded. "I think I'll go see him this morning. Might as well get the ball rolling. You'd better stay out of sight." Trace reached for his gun belt hanging on a hook near the back door of the hotel.

"I thought I'd mosey out to your farm and take a look see around. I'll check on Moses and Jimbo."

"Thanks. I haven't been out there for awhile."

\*   \*   \*

The word spread quickly that a camp meeting was coming to Anderson. The Negroes, their fear never far from the service, were excited and hopeful. It was a bright clear day with a nip of Fall in the air. It should prove to be a good night for the meeting.

The day before, to Trace's astonishment, an itinerant preacher showed up. He was an old man with white hair and beard. The wagon he was driving was weather worn and ramshackle, but the mule looked slick and well groomed. He pulled the wagon up to the livery and stepped down from the wagon, his smooth movements belying the age in his face.

"Howdy," the man greeted the stable owner.

"Howdy," Don Simpson answered. "What can I do for you, preacher?" He had read the faded letters on the wagon bed., "*REV. JOSHUA LEDBETTER*", and beneath that, "*Binging the Lord's Message to the Masses.*"

"I need a good resting place for my faithful friend here. Hiram is strong but he's plumb tuckered out. We been on the road for quite a spell."

"I got a nice stall in the back. Two bits a day. Oats extra. "Simpson was a man of few words, particularly when it came to strangers.

"That'll do. Give him a ration of oats today, then once in a while."

"How long you plan to stay in Anderson?" There was something about the man that nagged at him, but he couldn't put his finger on it.

"Well, sir, I don't know except I would like to get the folks together for a camp meeting. Who would I see about that?"

"The sheriff, I reckon. Name's Dawson. His office is on Main Street a couple of blocks from the hotel. You want your animal took care of right now?"

"Yes sir. I need to walk the kinks out of my legs." Ledbetter went back to the wagon and pulled it along side the livery. He removed Hiram's harness and led him to Simpson who was standing just outside the stable.

"Hiram won't cause you any trouble. He's a right agreeable mule."

Simpson grinned. "Yeah, they all are."

Sheriff Dawson rose from his desk when Reverand Ledbetter reached his office.

"What can I do for you, sir?"

"I'm Reverend Joshua Ledbetter." He held out his hand.

The sheriff resounded with a handshake. He was surprised at the man's firm grip.

"What can I do for you, Reverend?" He looked intently into the man's eyes but they told him nothing.

"Well, sir, I would like to hold a camp meeting here. Do I need to buy a permit or some kind of document?"

"Not necessary as long as I know what's going on. There's a vacant lot where the school house use to be before the Klanners burned it down. You're welcome to camp on it.

How long do you plan to stay in Anderson?"

"Don't know for sure. Depends on your people, I guess."

"The people are hungry for visitors and they will probably fill up your tent, if you have one."

"No I don't have a tent since mine was destroyed by a storm. My partner died about two months ago, and I haven't found anyone willing to share a poor preacher's lot."

"I'll try to round up a couple of the young men to help you. That is, if you don't mind using Negro help."

"No sir. We are all one color in God's eyes. I'll be much obliged for your help."

"I'll walk over to the camp site with you and you can see if it is suitable. We've cleaned it up and hauled all the debris away." The sheriff reached for his hat and the two men headed for the proposed campground.

\*     \*     \*

When Trace awoke from the long night's patrol, he found an old man with a white hair and a beard sitting in the chair in his room. "What the . . ."

The old man laughed. "If I can fool you, I can fool the Klanners."

Trace rubbed the sleep from his eyes. He stared at the man's face with a puzzled look on his own.

The man laughed again and recognition dawned. "Grady, what in the world are you doing in that git up.?"

Trace rose from the bed and the two men shook hands. Trace began dressing.

"You know during the war I wore a lot of hats. One of them was a preacher's. I thought this camp meeting would be a good place to *"hide out."*

"It couldn't be more appropriate under the circumstances. Say, how did you get the hair and beard and the wrinkles in your face?"

"Theater make up. One job I did, I worked with a bunch of actors for awhile, and they taught me how to look any way I want to look."

"That must have been an education!"

Grady grinned, his wrinkles crinkling up. "It was." Then he turned serious. "I called on Dawson. I don't think he recognized me. We went to the place where hey burned the schoolhouse and I'm going to use it for the campground."

"You mean you're actually gonna preach a sermon?"

"Wait and see." Grady promised.

\*     \*     \*

The preacher moved his wagon to the appointed place. He returned Hiram to the stable and hurried back to set up his meager props. A scarred walnut pulpit, two cane backed chairs a buckets of water for baptizing and two tin plates for the offering. The afternoon was drawing to a close and he needed to be prepared for the Klanners if they came. His revolver was in the pocket of his shabby black coat, his rifle and shot gun in the wagon.

The Reverend Ledbetter inspected his makeup, made a few repairs, washed his hands and combed his long white hair. He changed into a ragged but clean shirt and slipped into his black coat. He ran through the few religious passages he knew and hoped they would be enough to get through till the Klanners came, that is, if they did. He intended to quiz the audience to see how many were of a religious nature. That always took considerable time.

The Negroes were the first to arrive and stood off to one side. Most of them had brought chairs or benches. The young'uns were quiet and their well scrubbed faces shined in the growing dusk. The conversation was muted. A tall lighted candle was placed on the pulpit and Reverend Ledbetter pretended to be reading from the battered old Bible. The Negroes were orderly and respectful.

A few white people showed up and chose the other side of the yard. Ledbetter recognized Regina and Joe Hutchenson. John Michaels followed but there was no sign of Trace. The preacher knew Trace was on watch at the road leading into town from the south while the sheriff had men at the end of the road coming from the north.

Twilight quickly descended and Ledbetter stood in front of the crowd and held up his hands for silence. "Friends," he began. "I didn't rightly know about this town till I ran right into it. Been preaching at a country church t'other side of Brenham. My name is Reverend Joshua Ledbetter and I bring the word of God to all the unsaved. By a show of hands, how many of you have not been baptized'

Very few white hands went up but the Negroes show of hands was nearly all of them.

'I'm not sure I can get all of you done tonight for need to say a word about it before we begin. Now how many of you have heard about Jesus and how he was crucified for our sins?"

Almost every hand went up and muted *Amens* could be heard coming from the Negroes. One old white haired Negro man spoke up. "My old master, he tell us that story bout Jesus and how he come back to life. It be true, preacher?"

"Yes, brother it's true." Ledbetter began to tell the story of how Jesus came to die on the cross His voice carried through the crowd and he had their full attention. "And there you have it, my friends. Our Savior was dead. His battered lifeless body was taken to a tomb and placed there for the women to tend. But, we all know that he rose from the dead on the third day. The tomb was empty when the women came to prepare the body."

The preacher had just finished speaking when a young Negro boy of ten or twelve came running from the section of the road Trace was guarding. "They's comin', they's coming. Them Klanners is comin' and they's got they's heds covered with some kind a white sacks. And they's wearin' white coats."

The women screamed and the crowd began to panic. Ben Conner who had joined the group began to try and calm them down. "Find some cover and stay put," he told them. The area behind the school house was heavily wooded and he started in that direction. The Klanners had not reached the town due to the heavy rifle fire coming from both ends of the road. Trace and his men and the sheriff and his bunch had the Klanners in a cross fire. One of the Klanners tumbled from the saddle and lay still in the road.

The buckskin horse was wild eyed and the rider tried to calm him while shooting his revolver. The horse reared and the rider came tumbling from the saddle. Trace was on him in an instant and pulled him to his feet. He yanked the hood off his head and threw it on the ground. "Fred Collins." Trace spoke, his voice and actions tightly controlled.

The Klanners had been a small group, They decided that it was unhealthy in the area and spurred their horses to the west. They disappeared in a matter of minutes.

The sheriff and his men rode up and Dawson took one look at the scene before him.

"Fred Collins, I want to question you about the death of Alvin Burdette!"

# CHAPTER NINETEEN

THE SHERIFF TOOK COLLINS TO the jail and locked him in a cell. Collins was angry and kept up a up a barrage of denials, that he had nothing to do with Alvin Burdette's death.

"We found Alvin laying in the field and he was already dead. Why would I want to kill Alvin?"

"Maybe you saw a way to get the Burdette farm if Alvin was out of the picture," Dawson answered. "You know it is a good piece of land and was a prosperous place before the war."

"The Burdettes were my friends all except that turn coat Trace. Hell, we came to Grimes County and settled here at the same time."

"What would you say if I told you I have a witness that saw you kill Alvin?"

"I'd say you're a God damn liar!"

The sheriff's face blazed a bright red. "Hold your tongue or I'll forget I'm a lawman. We already know you're a Klanner and probably one of them that ruined Trace's crops."

"You can't prove that!"

""No, but the witness is ready to testify so let's hope you get a quick trial." Dawson turned the key in the lock and strode back into his office.

Trace had remained silent during the exchange between the sheriff and Collins. His temper was at the boiling point and he knew if Collins provoked him, he would lose control.

"Sheriff, I'm going to look for Regina and John. I saw them in the crowd for a second and then they vanished."

. "I'm putting a guard on this bird around the clock. Some of his Klanner friends might try to break him out. I might have to call on you later to help out but not unless it is absolutely necessary considering the bad blood between you two. You go ahead and check out the meeting place and see if you can get a handle on the dead man."

Trace nodded and headed for the meeting place. The crowd had dispersed and only the preacher remained.

"Howdy," he greeted Trace. "I think it's time I pulled out. Don't think anyone will blame me after what has happened. I'm sorry, Trace, I couldn't join in the fight, but I thought it would look unseemly for a man of the cloth to take part."

"Forget it. You did your part in drawing them out. Fred Collins is locked up and one was killed so I'd say we didn't do too bad. Has anyone identified the man?"

"I don't think so. They hauled him off to the undertaker's place." Grady scratched his face and neck. "I got to get this damn stuff off me. It itches like hell."

Trace laughed. "My what language for a man of the cloth. By the way where did you get the wagon and mule?"

"Got it in Brenham from the army post. I hope the wagon holds together till I can get it back there."

"Have you seen Regina and John? I caught a glimpse of them when the fight was over but they had disappeared when I got back to the place where I saw them."

"I think they went back to the hotel. Joe Hutcheson was with them. Trace, if you got any ideas about making Regina Lillijean's mother, you'd best get a move on."

Trace shook his head, "Grady, you should know that a refined lady like Regina would never consider marriage to me. I know she loves Lillijean but that is not enough to base a marriage on."

"That's a lot of hogwash. Regina is not a snob and I know she favors you. That's plain to see. I don't think she will marry Joe Hutcheson unless you completely ignore her."

The two men reached the hotel and found Regina, John and Joe in the lobby. When Regina saw Trace the worried look left her face to be replaced by a smile. "Oh Trace, I was worried about you. Are you all right?"

"Yes, I'm still in one piece." Trace watched her carefully. Maybe Grady and John were right. Maybe she did care for him. But none of his thoughts showed on his face. "John, we got Fred Collins locked up in jail on suspicion of murdering my brother."

John's eyes widened and he was flabbergasted. "Have you . . . have you got any proof?"

"Yes, there was a witness but I'm not sure he will testify."

Joe spoke up. "Do you want to tell me about it? Perhaps I can help."

"Thanks Joe, but I think I should come to your office in the morning. Say about nine o'clock?"

"Fine. I'll be expecting you. Now if you will excuse me, I think it's time I went home." Joe had seen the emotions that played out on Regina's face when Trace arrived. So that's the way the wind blew. He didn't want to lose Regina so he would just have to increase the pressure. She is an educated woman from a good family and he couldn't see her marrying a farmer. She would make an excellent lawyer's wife.

\*   \*   \*

Trace found the sheriff at Joe's office the next morning. Dawson's smile was tinged with irony. "Howdy, sheriff," Trace greeted the lawman.

"I'm glad you're here. Let's hope Joe has a solution for getting Collins to trial."

"Yeah. I sure would hate to turn that guy loose. He's a guilty as sin."

"Do you mind telling me who the witness is?" Joe asked.

Trace filled Joe in with the information that Moses had given him. "I know it's a weak case but . . ."

Joe shook his head. "I'm sorry, but I don't see any way to get a fair trial. Besides the judge would probably throw the case out of court for insufficient evidence. Oh, I know Moses is telling the truth, but putting a Negro on the stand would start a riot."

Trace's features hardened and a steely glint came into his eyes. "There's more than one way to skin a cat."

Grady had accompanied Trace to Joe's office. "Now, Trace, don't do anything foolish. There's always the chance he could be killed riding with the Klanners. Or ambushed or . . .", Grady left the sentence unfinished.

"Yeah, let the law handle it. You don't want to do anything that would put you in jeopardy. "Dawson added. "I guess I will have to turn Collins loose but not before I blister his hide with a good tongue lashing."

After leaving Joe's office, Trace decided against following the sheriff to the jail. "Best if I stay away from there."

"I know this is hard for you, pard, but your time will come. I can promise you that," Grady told Trace.

Trace nodded but said nothing. He had turned the situation over and over in his mind but saw no legal way to bring Collins to justice. There had to be something he could do to avenge Alvin's death. Then he remembered the Bible passages his mother had taught her sons. One seemed to leap out at him. *Vengeance is mine, said the Lord.* How many times had she quoted that passage to them when they were growing up. But it was awful hard to know that your brother was murdered and know who the murderer was and not be able to do anything about it.

"I'm leaving for Brenham in a little while," Grady broke into Trace's thoughts. "Might be gone a couple of days, I need to report to the lutenant."

"You think I should keep up the patrols?"

"No, let them slide for a few days. Give yourself a chance to do some serious courting."

In spite of himself, Trace's face colored a bit.

"I do need to spend more time with Lillijean. As for Regina, I'm not sure but what she might decide Joe is the *better catch.*"

"Trace Burdette, I would never believe you would let that stand in your way. You saw how she looked at you last night. And Hutcheson was there at the time. I'm sure he saw it, too."

\*     \*     \*

Regina took the baby from Alice and sat in the rocking chair. Lillijean looked up, her little rosebud mouth forming a smile. "You are a beautiful little girl, Lillijean, and your Aunt Regina loves you. Yes, she does." She tickled the baby on her little round belly and Lillijean wiggled with delight.

"You make a pretty picture," Trace said from the doorway.

Regina looked startled for a moment, then replied, "Thank you, sir."

Trace entered the room and saw that Alice was preparing to leave. He wondered how much longer she would nurse Lillijean. There were no living quarters but he could build a cabin or two on the farm. Perhaps Alice's husband would work for him. Come spring there would be plenty of work to get the crops planted. Regina would need help and he was hoping Maybelle would come to the farm; however, she might elect to stay at the hotel. *Whoa there! You're getting the cart before the horse. I need to find out how Regina feels about me* before I go making any plans.

"Would you like to hold her?" Regina watched the emotions flit across Trace's face. *Why he's afraid to hold her.* "She won't break." She stood up and placed the baby in Trace's arms. Why don't you sit in the rocker awhile. It's comfortable and if you rock her she will probably fall asleep."

As Regina had predicted, Lillijean was soon sleeping peacefully. She took the baby from Trace and placed her in her cradle.

Trace looked down at the baby, his mind racing with unspoken thoughts. Should he tell Regina the truth about his marriage and that he was not Lillijean's biological father? If and it was a big if, Regina accepted his proposal, then he would divulge the truth.

Trace reached out and took Regina's hand. He led her to the rocking chair. She looked up, her eyes full of questions." Regina, I want you to know that I care deeply for you." Her face broke into a big smile and she started to rise from her chair. Trace motioned her to remain seated. "No, please wait until I finish." There didn't seem to be any way except straight out. "You know I came back to Texas to claim the farm Alvin left to me. I met Anne and John. I could tell something was troubling Anne, and she finally confided in me. She was expecting Alvin's baby. We married to protect her and, in a way, Alvin."

Regina gasped. "Then . . . then Lillijean is not your daughter?"

"No, but I promised I would take care of her and raise her like she was my own."

Regina's eyes were moist and she whispered, "Oh Trace, what a burden you have been carrying. Does John know?"

"Yes. He also knows how I feel about you." Trace sat down on the edge of the bed as if telling Regina the truth had drained him.

Regina arose from the rocker and went to Trace. He stood and she reached out to him. Taking her in his arms he held her tightly. Her face buried in his shoulder, Regina spoke softly." I care for you too, Trace." She lifted her head and he kissed her. It was a tender kiss without any of the passion he kept under control.

'Are you ready for the next question?" he asked, still holding her in his arms.

"I . . . I think so."

"Regina, will you marry me?

"Yes, yes, I'll marry you, Trace." Regina was overjoyed. This man she loved returned her love and wanted to be her husband.

"What about Joe Hutcheson?"

"Joe proposed but I did not accept his proposal. Joe is a fine man, but I cannot marry him when it is you I love."

Trace tightened his hold on Regina and kissed her again. This time she could feel the desire he kept under control. When the kiss finally ended, Regina was breathless. Her face flamed with the thoughts that ran through her mind.

Trace saw that Regina was flustered and grinned. He'd bet there was passion under that refined exterior. Then he thought of Anne and their make believe marriage. Should he tell Regina the marriage had never been consummated? Somehow he wanted her to know how much he respected Anne and loved her in a way different than his love for Regina.

"There's something I want to tell you. It may shock you but I want you to know." He cleared his throat and swallowed hard. "Regina my marriage to Anne was . . . was never consummated."

At this revelation Regina was speechless. Of course Anne had been carrying Alvin's baby, but still . . . Respect. Trace had respected Anne and played the part well. Regina would never have guessed they were not man and wife in every way. She felt proud that she had agreed to marry a man of such principles.

"Well, it's about time." John Michaels stood in the hallway in front of their door.

Another rosy blush stained Regina's cheeks and she started to move out of Trace's arms but he held her tight. "No you don't young lady. John this lovely lady has agreed to marry me."

"Now that's good news. When will the nuptials take place?"

"We haven't gotten that far," Regina replied.

*     *     *

Regina and Trace talked again after supper. This time they were sitting in the parlor. Trace thought of the times he had seen Regina with Joe. It came to him again what a lucky man he was. She had agreed to live on the farm with him. He knew it was a far cry from what she was used to, but he would do all he could to make it easier for her.

"Do you think Alice will come to the farm to nurse the baby?" Trace asked.

"I don't know. She has two little boys and I'm sure she wouldn't want to leave them."

"Maybe her husband would consider helping me with the cabins I want to build." Trace had already decided to build two cabins and later on a bunkhouse. "As soon as we get the cabins finished, they could move in. It will soon be time to get the ground ready for spring planting."

"What about Maybelle? I'd really like her to help me with the cooking and household chores. Especially till I get used to the routine." Regina could not help being apprehensive about the responsibility of running the household.

"If she is agreeable, we can make room for her. But she may want to stay at the hotel."

"That's true," Regina replied.

"Don't worry sweetheart. We will find somebody to help you."

Regina smiled. Already he was using endearments and they had been engaged less than a day. *He is going to be a wonderful husband, and I'm so glad we found each other.*

They were sitting on the settee and he put his arm around her shoulders. Don't you think it's time to set the date?"

"Yes, but I will need some time to get a trousseau together and to write to my brother. Not that they will come since Nancy is expecting."

"And I will need some time to get the house and cabins livable. And there's the paper work that is required when the Negroes work for you. I guess Joe will draw up the necessary documents. Speaking of Joe . . . ." Trace left the sentence unfinished. and looked to Regina for the answer.

Regina had completely forgotten about Joe "Joe is coming to call tomorrow night. I will tell him then."

"Do you want me to hang around or . . . I could go out on patrol." Trace didn't envy Joe Hutcheson. He was losing the one woman in Anderson who would have made him the perfect wife.

"I'll leave that up to you. I want to tell him in private. I think that will be easier for both of us."

Joe was dressed exceptionally nice the next evening when he came to call. Regina, too, had taken extra care with her appearance. Her brown bengaline gown with its ecru trim highlighted her brown eyes and fair skin.

After greeting John and spending a few minutes with him, Regina asked Joe if he would like to go into the parlor. He agreed and they settled down for what he hoped would be a fruitful evening.

Regina fidgeted with her handkerchief while they made small talk—the weather, the end of the epidemic and finally the baby. She should come right to the point. "Joe, I have enjoyed our evenings together. You are a delightful companion and kept me from forgetting my family—the theater, and other social activities that are so missing here."

"There's no reason we can't go to San Antonio a couple of times a year. I don't want to bury you in this small town."

"Regina shook her head. "I'm sorry to break this to you in this way, but it's best if I tell you right now."

Joe had a sinking feeling in the pit of his stomach. True, Regina had turned his proposal down, but he thought in time she might change her mind. He knew Trace Burdette was in the picture but . . .

Regina stood and walked to the table in the center of the room. She turned, Joe had risen and stood in front of her.

"I'm sorry Joe but I am going to marry Trace Burdette."

"Is it because of the baby?" he asked. "I know you love the little girl and have helped take care of her since she was born."

"No, Trace and I love each other. I'll admit I'm overjoyed to be able to help raise Lillijean. She's very precious to me."

Joe picked up his hat which was laying on the table. "I guess there is no more to day except to give you my best wishes. Trace is a fine man, and I'm sure you will be very happy."

# CHAPTER TWENTY

WORD SOON GOT AROUND THAT the school teacher was going to marry Trace Burdette. The ladies in the congregation of the church Regina attended were all aflutter. There were those who said he was marrying her just to have a mother for his child. Still others said it was a love match because you could see it in their faces. Regina ignored the skeptical remarks and thanked the others for their best wishes.

"Trace, you know I have an aunt and uncle in Marshall?" Regina said. They were in the parlor talking over the wedding plans.

'Yes, I remember you mentioned something about staying with them before you came to Anderson."

"I want to write them and invite them to the wedding. I'm not sure they will come, but I feel I should ask them."

"That's a good idea. You should have family with you on your wedding day."

Since Regina had no close friends after Anne's death, she would ask her Aunt Martha to be her attendant. Grady would be Trace's best man. It was to be a simple wedding with John, Alice and Maybelle attending. The nuptials would be held in the parsonage parlor.

"Don't you think we should set the date?" Trace asked.

"It will take me awhile to get my things together. I've sent to Indiana for my hope chest.'"

"I'm sorry Regina that I can't offer you a big house with servants," Trace said ruefully.

"I'm not marrying a house Trace. I'm marrying you."

"We will have that big house someday. I promise." Trace vowed. He put his arms around her and kissed her gently on the lips.

The couple talked about a date for the wedding and settled on a Saturday afternoon six weeks away. "That will give me some time to whip things into shape at the farm."

*       *       *

Trace had saved the money the army paid him. He spent most of his time repairing and renovating the farm house. Regina finally convinced him to let her tap into her trust fund for new bedroom furniture. It was made of local walnut and waxed to a satin finish. The armoire, dresser and bed took up most of the room. Regina managed to find space for Lillijean's cradle. She would have her own room when she was older. New curtains and coverlet in shades of blue and green complemented the dark furniture and polished floors.

The two cabins Trace wanted to build would be some distance away from the main house in a grove of oak trees. Each cabin would consist of three small rooms and a front and back porch. The tenants would be responsible for the furniture and it did not surprise anyone when the Negro population provided most of the necessities. Some pieces were handmade, others repaired from broken parts.

Grady was taking the patrols while Trace was occupied with the activity at the farm. He came off a late night patrol with the news that Fred Collins had been killed in a raid on a Negro settlement near Tyler. "It's funny how justice seems to find a way short of the court room." Grady commented.

""Now Alvin can rest in peace," Trace replied.

Trace went into town the next day to purchase supplies for the farm. His first stop was the hotel. He found Regina upstairs with Alice who was nursing Lillijean. Alice smiled and dropped her head when Trace kissed Regina. "Trace," Regina chastised him.

Trace grinned and answered, "Better get used to it lady." In a complete change of subject he asked, "When's dinner? I'm about starved."

"Now isn't that just like a man?" Regina pretended to be upset. "Always thinking about their stomachs."

After a heavy noon meal, Trace headed for the sawmill He had figured out how much lumber he would need for the cabins. He also needed some trim to replace what had been broken or ruined by neglect. The sawmill was operated by a man named James Parsons. Most people called him Big

Jim because of his size. He was a tall man and would probably weight over two hundred pounds.

"Howdy Burdette," Parsons greeted Trace. There was no hint of animosity in his tone.

"Howdy, Jim. I need some lumber for a couple of cabins I want o build on my farm."

Surprise flickered across Big Jim's face. "You figure to rent them to the Negroes in exchange for them helping you on the farm?"

"No, I won't rent them. They will be part of the compensation." Trace watched Big Jim closely for signs of prejudice. There were none.

"Bout time we put that war behind us." Parsons said. "Been enough killiin' and bloodshed. And with them Klanners running wild, we need to stick together."

*    *    *

While Trace was busy with the work at the farm, Regina began her preparations for the wedding. The first thing to do was write to Uncle Edward and Aunt Martha. And David and Nancy. Oh, how David will fuss and fume! Both letters were written and sent out on the next mail run.

Then there was the matter of her trousseau. Regina did not want an elaborate wedding dress and decided on a gown she had never worn. The cream silk with its lace collar and long lace trimmed sleeves would be just right for the weather. Since the wedding would not be in the church, Regina chose to forgo a veil and wear a hat she had purchased when the dress was made. It was a frothy concoction of ivory silk and satin trimmed with tiny pink silk roses. Regina was glad there would be no need for a going away outfit or day gowns that would have been essential in Indianapolis.

Regina blushed as she inspected her undergarments thinking that Trace would see her in them. Her petticoats, corsets, chemises, and pantalets were all lace trimmed and in good condition. She also had satin slippers she had never worn. *I could use a new gown and robe.* Perhaps she could purchase something at the dressmakers. Regina knew she would need serviceable calico frocks at the farm but they could wait until later.

Two weeks later a letter came from Aunt Martha. They would be delighted to come to the wedding. They would arrive on the stage two days before the happy event. Of course Regina had not heard from her brother and sister-in-law. The distance was too great. She knew her brother would object strenuously to her marriage to a farmer. So be it.

*     *     *

The work on the cabins progressed rapidly. They would be ready for their new tenants before the wedding. Trace was hoping Maybelle would decide to come to the farm. If she stayed at the hotel and worked for John, then he would have to find someone else to help Regina. He did not want her to do all of the heavy work involved in living on a farm.

As Trace was working on the inside of one of the cabins, Ben O'Connor appeared in the doorway. "Hello, Mr. Burdette. I heard you were building the cabins. Is there anything I can do to help/"

"Hello Ben. If you want to help, grab a hammer and some nails."

"Yes sir," Ben answered as he picked up the hammer and fished some nails out of the keg. 'Tell me what you want me to do."

'The trim around the windows and doors should be done so that we can whitewash the inside."

The two men worked in silence for several minutes. "Mr. Burdette did you know that Mr. Hutcheson is going to let me read law with him?'

"No, I didn't know that. Joe Hutcheson is a fine lawyer and you couldn't find a better teacher," Trace pounded a nail into place.

"Yes, I'm really very lucky that he is willing to let me learn from him. I feel that's the best way I can help my people. You know what I mean, Mr. Burdette?"

"Yes, Ben I do. It's mighty fine of you to feel that way. I wish you all the success in the world."

"Thank you, sir."

"Massa Trace, here be the whitewash you asked fur. You want Rufus and me to start in the other cabin seein' as to how it be finished?" Moses and his grandson were carrying pails of the thick white liquid.

"Yes you can start on it but Moses you take it easy. Rome wasn't built in a day." He could see the questions in their eyes. Trace grinned because he knew the Negroes had no idea what he was talking about.

"Mr. Burdette," Ben returned Trace's grin. He was probably the only Negro in Anderson that knew what Trace meant. He put his hammer in the collection of saws and other tools. "That delivery man is back and I'll catch a ride back to town."

"Thanks for your help, Ben. When you feel the need to get out of town, just head for the Burdette farm. You are always welcome."

*   *   *

Trace and Grady headed for the saloon. A hard day's work called for a drink. The place was crowded with townsmen who felt the need for something stronger than water or coffee. Both men ordered beer. It wasn't cold since there was no ice left from the previous winter. But it was wet and tasted good to Trace and Grady after a hard day's work on the cabins.

Grady saw the men at the poker table and recognized two of them as the Jackson brothers. At the same time, one of them looked up and saw Grady. He nudged his brother and Grady could almost hear what he was saying. "There's the dirty dog that turned traitor on us."

By this time, the other men in the saloon had heard Jackson's accusation. Grady pushed his beer away and turned toward the poker table. "Hold on pard," Trace cautioned.

"There's two of them," Grady answered.

One of the Jackson brothers had lost a leg in the war and used a crutch in order to keep his balance. Evidently the Jackson's had been drinking heavily because he was using the crutch. Both of them met Grady halfway between the gamblers and the bar.

"You dirty traitor," the cripple challenged Grady.

"I don't want to fight you," Grady replied. "Let's forget about it and save all of us some grief."

"Forget about it? You might want to forget it, but I got a long memory," he said as he swung the crutch at Grady.

Grady stepped backward but the crutch caught him on the shoulder. A bolt of pain ripped through his arm and he stumbled. Trace grabbed his other arm and kept him from falling. The pain began to subside but a numbness took its place. It was his gun arm and Grady did a cross draw and his revolver appeared in his left hand. Jackson swatted again with the crutch and the gun went flying out of Grady's hand.

The other Jackson took a swing at Trace. Trace ducked and the man's fist missed its target. By this time Trace had lost his temper and he returned the man's swing with a solid punch to his midsection. He grunted and doubled over. Trace took advantage of Jackson's brief pause to land another blow to his chin. Trace was no stranger to bar room brawls and could hold his own with the best of them.

"What the hell is going on here?" the sheriff's voice interrupted the fight. He appeared in the doorway, revolver in his hand.

"We just came in for a drink and these boys jumped us." Trace told him.

The sheriff nodded. "You Jacksons always cause trouble. I'm advising you to leave town and don't come back anyways soon." He waved his gun toward Grady. "You better see the doc about that arm. It's going to be mighty sore when the feeling comes back."

"You gonna arrest them, sheriff?" one of the bystanders asked.

"No, if they didn't start the fight, there's no call to arrest them."

"Well, you should. After all they are dirty Yankees, both of them."

The sheriff holstered his weapon. "The war is over, mister. You'd best keep that in mind."

The man mumbled something that sounded like "Maybe for you but there's lots of us don't think so."

"Grady, we need to get you to the doctor. Can't have you with a bad arm at the wedding. You're responsible for the ring until I put it on Regina's finger."

\*     \*     \*

The time passed swiftly and Regina found herself waiting for the stage to arrive. Uncle Edward and Aunt Martha should be on it. The wedding was two days away and Regina had a case of *nerves*. Maybe she should postpone the wedding. Aunt Martha would understand. She was not sure about Uncle Edward. He was very conservative with his money and would think the trip was a waste. And Trace. What would he think? He probably would think she didn't love him. But she did, Lord. She loved him with all her heart. She couldn't do that to him.

"Stage is coming. Stage is coming."

Regina patted her hair which she wore in a neat chignon and smoothed her skirts before she left the lobby. The stage came to a stop with the jingle of harnesses and dust. Regina caught a glimpse of a woman's face peering out the window. Aunt Martha and Uncle Edward had arrived. The woman was helped out of the stage first and she saw Regina immediately. They ran into each others arms, both crying tears of joy. Regina realized just how much she had missed her family.

"Oh, it's so good to see you," Regina told the plump little woman.

"Yes, dear. We missed you after you left to come here but it pleased us both that you wrote often," Aunt Martha said. as they entered the hotel.

Uncle Edward, a dour faced man in a rusty black suit followed carrying their luggage. "What about this young man you're going to marry?" Uncle Edward spoke up.

"Trace is at the farm today but he will be home for supper."

John was in the lobby and greeted Regina's relatives. "I have a nice room ready for you," he told them. "Regina, it's room number 104."

Regina lead the way while her aunt and uncle followed her up the stairs. She stopped in front of the door with a large 104 painted on it. She ushered her relatives in and saw that John had changed the coverlet and curtains to pretty flowered ones. The floor had been recently polished as had the dresser, the rocker, straight chair and lamp tables.

"Here you are," Regina waved her hand around the room. "John has done a marvelous job with this room. You know, when cowboys, stage drivers and other working men use the rooms they can get . . . well. you know."

"Yes dear. It's a lovely room and I'm sure we will be quite comfortable." Aunt Martha sighed.

Regina knew her aunt and uncle too were probably exhausted from the long stage ride. "You need to rest before supper. There's fresh water in the bowl and clean towels if you want to freshen up. Come down whenever you are ready. We usually eat supper around six o'clock. I guess that's my doing. We had *dinner* at home at six."

"How are your brother and his wife?" Aunt Martha inquired. "You said in your letters that she is in the family way."

"Yes, they are expecting their first child in December. I think it is difficult for Nancy but she wants a child so desperately."

"I hope everything goes all right with her," Aunt Martha said as she unpacked her portmanteau. "Do you think this dress is suitable for your wedding?" she asked. She held up a gown of blue bengaline with a white lace collar.

"Yes, it's very pretty and the color is perfect for you. It matches your eyes."

Aunt Martha smiled and patted Regina's hand. "You are such a sweet girl. I hope your young man appreciates you."

Supper was a festive affair and Maybelle had out done herself with the food. There was fried chicken, baked ham, mounds of mashed potatoes, and other vegetables and relishes. For dessert she served big wedges of apple pie. The men folk did justice to the meal while Regina and Aunt Martha kept their appetites in check.

"Miss Regina," Maybelle said as she served coffee to accompany the pie, "I have your wedding cake almost done. Just need to put on the finishing touches."

There was to be a small reception after the ceremony and Mrs. Foster insisted on hosting it in the parsonage. Of course there would be no alcoholic beverages but a fruit punch would be served. Regina could not help but think of the elaborate weddings she had attended in Indianapolis. It didn't matter at all. She would be just as married as if all the trimmings were in place. She was happy to marry the man she loved and who loved her.

The wedding day was clear and bright. Fall had come and the leaves were beginning to turn. The golden sunshine and the deep blue sky painted a picture to rival the paintings in Regina's books. She awoke early and lay listening to the birds outside her window. She felt rested but knew she would be jittery all day and she refused to think about her wedding night. She was ignorant of men and their passions, but she was sure Trace would be a gentle lover. It was herself she was worried about and how she would respond. No use to worry about it. Trace would understand and be patient. She jumped out of bed and began dressing.

Trace and Grady had been downstairs for some time before Regina appeared. Grady had been ribbing Trace and Trace was beginning to tire of it. Regina's presence put a stop to the ribald remarks. The two men greeted her and Trace asked if she wanted breakfast. He had not eaten and had been waiting for her.

Aunt Martha and Uncle Edward appeared and Maybelle served breakfast. Regina was too excited to eat and she noticed Trace did not have his usual hearty appetite. Was he regretting his proposal? She felt a moment of panic. *What if he leaves and doesn't show up for the wedding. I would be mortified. That would break my heart. Trace is an honorable man and would not do such a thing.*

With breakfast out of the way, Regina went to see Lillijean. She had been fed and bathed and Alice was dressing her. She smiled when she saw Regina and tried to wiggle away from Alice. "No, you don't, little girl." When she was clothed, Regina took her and sat in the rocker. There was a problem. Who was going to take care of Lillijean during the wedding ceremony and reception? Trace planned to take Regina to the farm after the wedding and they wanted to be alone.

"Miz Regina, you want I should stay here and mind the baby? I can stay the night, too."

"Oh Alice, you are the answer to my prayers. Trace and I are going to the farm after the ceremony."

Alice grinned, showing a missing tooth. "I know you don't want no baby around on your wedding night."

Regina blushed. She loved Lillijean but . . .

Regina arrived at the parsonage with Aunt Martha and Uncle Edward who agreed to give the bride away. Trace, Grady and John were waiting in the parlor. Somehow there were fresh flowers for Regina's bouquet and the table that held the wedding cake and punch bowl. She was resplendent in the cream silk dress which emphasized her flawless complexion. Her shiny light brown hair was done in a chignon with the fancy hat settled firmly on her head.

Trace and Grady were attired in black broadcloth suits, their white shirts a startling contrast. Both men sported fresh haircuts. Their black boots were polished to a rich luster. The ever present gun belts were missing and Regina breathed a sigh of relief.

Maybelle arrived and was seated in the parlor. The reverend's wife was a busy little bee checking all the details to make sure everything was the way it should be.

The ceremony went off without a hitch. Trace placed the heavy gold band with its intricate engraving on Regina's finger. "I now pronounce you husband and wife. You may kiss the bride." Trace took Regina in his arms and kissed her soundly. She blushed from the roots of her hair to below the lace trim on her gown. The reception was a pleasant interlude but the happy couple soon excused themselves to begin the trip to the farm.

Trace and Regina reached the farm as the sun sunk slowly in the west. The golden rays spread out and were underlined with orange clouds. Slowly the sky turned to lavender and twilight covered the land. Trace and Regina watched from the bedroom window as twilight gave way to total darkness. Trace lit the candles on the dresser and surveyed his bride. He knew she was nervous, perhaps even a little afraid of what was going to happen.

Regina, clad in the new gown and robe, stood in the middle of the room. Trace had removed his coat and shirt. He pulled off the top half of his under drawers and Regina saw his chest was covered with a patch of tight black curls. He took her in his arms. Lord! She was as stiff as a board. "Relax honey. I won't do anything you don't want me to do." He kissed her with controlled passion and she responded by putting her arms around him. He kissed her again and this time she began a timid search of his lips. He picked her up and carried her to the bed.

Regina felt strange emotions surging through her body. She loved this man who was now her husband and he would teach her the things she needed to know. She felt him settle on the other side of the bed. She slipped the robe off and let it fall to the floor.

He turned on his side and pulled her into his arms. His skin was hot to the touch and she tangled her fingers in the curls on his chest. "I love you." he whispered in her ear. She smiled and said "I love you Trace Burdette."

THE END